S.T.E.A.L.T.H.
ICE BREAKER

JASON ROHAN

nosy
crow

First published in the UK in 2022 by Nosy Crow Ltd
The Crow's Nest, 14 Baden Place,
Crosby Row, London, SE1 1YW, UK

Nosy Crow Eireann Ltd
44 Orchard Grove, Kenmare,
Co Kerry, V93 FY22, Ireland

Nosy Crow and associated logos are trademarks and/or registered
trademarks of Nosy Crow Ltd

ISBN: 978 1 83994 340 9

A CIP catalogue record for this book is available from the
British Library.

Printed and bound in the UK by Clays Ltd, Elcograf S.p.A.
Typeset by Tiger Media

Papers used by Nosy Crow are made from wood grown in sustainable
forests

MIX
Paper from
responsible sources
FSC® C018072

1 3 5 7 9 10 8 6 4 2

www.nosycrow.com

To Dominica, for relighting the fuse

09:34

"This is unacceptable, Mr Quinn."

Quinn sniffed. "Madam Chair, I don't give a fig if you accept it or not. That's my evidence."

"You cannot simply shrug your shoulders and deny all knowledge of this matter. We are talking about a billion pounds of public money wasted and you, as a senior Secret Service officer, are still a public servant." The Chair's voice was growing louder as she spoke. "It must be accounted for and that is why this Parliamentary select committee is sitting." She slid her glasses down her nose and glared at the older man. "What is more, I strongly advise you to watch your tone before this committee holds you in contempt."

Quinn looked at his watch.

"Are we keeping you from something, Mr Quinn? Do you have somewhere else you'd rather be?" The Chair could scarcely hide her irritation.

"I do have a hot bacon roll waiting for me, since you ask," Quinn replied. "Are we done?"

"Certainly not!"

Quinn sighed and settled back into his chair. It was going to be another long day. He was facing the open end of a long, horseshoe-shaped table behind which a dozen suits sat, staring at him. The defence select committee was meeting for a third day in the Wilson Room, on the first floor of Portcullis House, across from Big Ben and the Houses of Parliament. Its purpose was to determine what had happened to Project MANDROID.

The Vice Chair cleared his throat for dramatic effect. "If I may, Madam Chair," he drawled. "Perhaps a recap would be helpful, to allow Mr Quinn to assist in filling any gaps in my knowledge?" He noisily tapped his notepad.

Quinn slumped further into his seat and rested his chin on his hand. The last thing he needed was another windbag MP, in love with the sound of his own voice, grandstanding for an audience of one.

"You, Mr Quinn, work for British Intelligence, and your involvement here began with the disappearance of a Ministry of Defence scientist. That particular gentleman was working on a stealth weapon—"

"Transport vehicle," Quinn interjected.

The Vice Chair glowered at Quinn. "How many 'transport vehicles' do you know that could destroy two

2

RAF Typhoon fighter aircraft? I will continue. A stealth weapon, developed at considerable cost to His Majesty's government, I might add, and kept at a classified location. In the course of your investigation, you learned that a plot was underway to steal that stealth weapon and to smuggle it out of the country, for sale to a hostile government."

"At least you were paying attention," Quinn said.

"The lead scientist, it turns out, had been captured by an unknown enemy force. You went to negotiate a ransom payment and allowed yourself to be taken, too, so you could gain inside knowledge of the gang."

"Yep. Regular hero, that's me."

"But the enemy was able to storm the secret base, obtain the weapon, load it on to an aeroplane and was in the process of flying it out of the country."

"And that's when your MOD geniuses decided to send two Typhoons to blast it out of the sky," Quinn said. "While I was on board."

"And in the ensuing firefight, both RAF jets and the Hercules transport were destroyed."

The Chair leaned forward. "Which leads us back to the original question of, what happened to this MANDROID weapon?" she snapped.

3

"And I told you," Quinn said, "it was destroyed when the transport plane crashed into the English Channel. It's gone. Drowned. Washed away. Under the sea. In Davy Jones's locker. Feeding the fishes. Finding Nemo."

"Then why have we found no wreckage? The Typhoons, the Hercules; parts of all three aircraft have washed up on the shore and the remaining airframes recovered, but for this device, nothing."

Quinn was losing the little patience he had. "The experts have already told you, nothing could have survived that crash."

"*You* did."

Quinn paused, his eyes narrow. "That's different. I jumped."

"But you take my point. If you somehow escaped intact..."

"You're forgetting a very important detail," Quinn said.

"Oh?"

"The nuclear bomb. It was in the hold of the MANDROID vehicle, right? The Hercules crashed, broke apart, everything went down. The rescue sub recovered the bomb."

"Yes, it was on the sea bed."

"After being in the plane."

"Is there a point to this?" The Chair set her pen down and directed a hard stare at Quinn.

"That stealth device was the most advanced craft of its kind in the world. I'm clearly no technical expert and can't tell you half of what went into it, or what it could do, but I know there was a lot of nanotechnology in there, which is what made it change its shape into different kinds of vehicle, from tractor to hovercraft."

"We've all seen the presentation," droned the Vice Chair.

"Then you'll also know that tiny particles held together have a tendency to fall apart when they're no longer actively controlled. Surely it's obvious that when the thing crashed, it crumbled to dust and what didn't end up as silt got washed away on the currents. That's why there's no wreckage. You shouldn't need me to spell that out for you."

A wave of consternation rippled around the table. Foreheads touched amid the purr of low voices as the suits conferred.

Quinn closed his eyes and waited.

A decision reached, the Chair motioned for silence. "We'll need some time to consider this development," she announced. "The hearing is adjourned for today."

* * *

"Over here, sir!"

Quinn strode over to the black Range Rover waiting opposite on the Victoria Embankment and eased into the passenger side, taking care to scoop up the foil-wrapped package on the seat before he sat down.

In the driver's seat was Simon Burgess, former Royal Marine, survivor of the assault on MANDROID base, and now the first recruit to Quinn's new team.

"Think they fell for it?" Burgess asked, easing the car into traffic.

"Let's hope so," Quinn said. "It's a lot easier to believe than the truth." He unwrapped the package and sank his teeth into the now-cold bacon roll.

09:45

Eight miles to the west, at The Most Sacred Heart High School in Richmond, the bell rang to announce change of lessons.

Chairs scraped noisily, accompanied by the buzz of chatter, as Class 8F packed up to move from English to science.

Sam Evans shouldered his Iron Man backpack and fell in line beside Arun Lal, his best friend, as they made for the door.

"I was thinking, yeah, that the basic plot of *Civil War* and *Black Widow* is the same," Sam said.

"Really?" Arun said, shuffling forward. "In what way?"

"Well, in both films, the main threat is a bunch of specially trained agents who can take down whole countries and the heroes have to go to Russia to stop them."

"I suppose," Arun agreed, heading into the corridor. "Of course, there's a lot—"

"And with *Black Widow* and *Winter Soldier*, both films have a cyborg assassin as the bad guy, and have a big aerial battle at the end. Uh-oh." Sam stopped as an older boy cut across to block his path.

The stream of pupils walking past pressed itself closer to the opposite wall, as if repelled by a force field.

The older boy pointed at Sam's head. "Whoa, check that dead trim! What did they use to cut your hair? A lawnmower? Your hairline looks like the McDonald's logo." He laughed at his own wit.

Sam froze.

"Leave it, Kyle," Arun said, without looking up. "We're not worth it."

"Who's talking to you?" said a voice from behind him. It belonged to Josh, another older boy who hung out with Kyle.

Josh landed a firm grip on Sam's backpack and yanked it off his shoulders. He held it up and pointed at the picture of Iron Man printed on the fabric.

"What's this? Are you three years old or something? Wanna play fetch?"

He lobbed the backpack over his shoulder.

"Oops. I hope there was nothing breakable in there."

"I know something that's gonna break in a minute." It

was a girl's voice, from behind Josh.

He whirled around to see a 12-year-old girl holding up the backpack.

"Who threw this?" Donna Critchlow demanded.

"Uh, it was him," Josh said, taking a step back and pointing at Kyle.

"No, it wasn't, you liar," Kyle protested.

Donna set the backpack down, pushed out her lower jaw and narrowed her eyes. "Which do you think is going to be the bigger embarrassment for you: getting stomped by a Year Eight, or getting stomped by a Year Eight girl?" she said.

"I'm late for class," Josh said. He scurried away, grabbing Kyle as he went.

"Yeah, that's right," Donna called after the departing boys. "Walk away."

Sam breathed a huge sigh of relief, opened his arms and moved towards Donna to give her a great big hug of gratitude. She raised her index finger, stopping him dead.

"One: respect my personal space, if you know what's good for you. Two: I don't know you. Three: you're welcome. Now, take your pack and let's go to class."

Sam nodded, his face pink with a wash of emotions.

"She's so amazing," he whispered to Arun.

Donna strode past, smiling to herself, and pretended not to hear.

09:58

At British Secret Intelligence Service headquarters, Quinn fished the scrunched bacon roll foil wrapper from his pocket and tossed it across the empty room. It bounced off a whiteboard, pinged against the window and dropped into a waste basket.

"Yes," he said, giving himself a fist pump. "Still got it."

Eight workstations were set up in the office, with laptop docking stations and flat-screen monitors, although none were in use.

Quinn sighed inwardly. Not long ago, this room was a hive of activity where his crack team of operatives tracked threats to national security and hunted terror cells. That was before they had all been exposed as traitors, lured into betraying their country with the promise of easy money. And now Quinn had to start again and recruit a new team, only this time he would be less trusting.

"Sir?" Burgess came in with a laptop bag, set it down and unzipped it. "Is there anywhere in particular you want me to sit?"

"You're good where you are," Quinn said. "Those two desks, next to you, they're reserved."

Burgess brightened. "They are? You mean, you've got two more team members? When do I meet them?"

Quinn's mouth twisted in a sour expression. "We'll get to that. They're a little on the … raw side."

"Where are they now? In the building?"

"No, I've sent them far away, where they can't be questioned by the select committee."

Burgess tilted his head. "Permission to speak freely, sir?"

"You're not in the Marines any more, son. Spit it out."

"It's just … you don't sound very confident about the quality of these new recruits."

Quinn paused. "Let's say it was a limited pool and they were the best I could get. Don't ask how bad the rest must have been."

"Can you stop fidgeting?" Sunny Patel hissed. "You're making us look bad."

"I can't help it," replied Andrew Moss, sitting opposite Sunny. He wriggled again. "This vest's too tight. It's cutting into my armpit. And it's pinching my nipple."

Sunny reached over and loosened a strap on the body

armour. "Is that better?"

"Somewhat."

"I told you, it's better to put it on first and then tighten it up, not the other way round. See? Mine fits perfectly."

A tall, lean soldier, in full combat gear, knelt in the aisle of the train carriage next to them. "Is all in order?" he asked. "I can help if you are not used to wearing this." He smiled with a flash of white teeth and held out his hand.

"I can manage just fine," Moss said, squirming away. "It's been a while since I last wore one of these. I'm out of practice, is all."

"Naturally," the soldier said. He looked at Sunny. "And, Ms Patel, would you like me to help you with anything? Anything at all?"

Sunny felt her cheeks grow warm and lowered her head to hide it. "No, thank you, Dietmar. But I'll be sure to let you know if that changes."

"Please, call me Didi." The tall Austrian straightened up and headed down the carriage.

Moss pulled a face. "Ugh. Since when did you know his name was Dietmar? I thought he was just Corporal Mertens."

"I asked him, back in Zurich. He's nice."

Moss scowled. "I don't trust him. I see him making goo-goo eyes at you, turning on the charm."

Sunny laughed. "What? No, he's not. Wait, are you … jealous?"

"What, of that great German sausage? That'll be the day."

"He's Austrian." Sunny decided to change the subject. "You know, when Mr Quinn offered us a romantic train journey across the Alps as a first assignment, this wasn't what I had in mind, riding shotgun in an armoured train full of Austrian Special Forces."

Moss smiled and leaned closer. "I don't know. We got some skiing in … and a hot tub … plus some fondue. Now it's the work bit, watching and learning how the pros do things."

Sunny reached across to slide open a peephole on the metal-clad outer wall. A sliver of purest blue sky sitting atop a frosted crag of mountain glided past. "And we still get the view."

"Uh-uh. Please, that must stay closed." A female soldier with a short blonde bob stood in the gangway, wagging her finger.

"Maybe not," Sunny muttered to herself, and closed the slit.

"Hey, Petra," Moss said to the stern-looking figure. "This is a lot of security we have here. Can I ask why? What cargo are we carrying?"

The soldier's glare melted into a smile. "They didn't tell you, before sending you all this way?"

"No." Moss shook his head.

"Good. Let's keep it that way." She spun on her heel and marched away.

As soon as she was out of earshot, Sunny rounded on Moss. "How did you know her name was Petra?" she demanded. "I thought she was just Corporal Friedrich."

"I asked her. Same as you and Dodo."

"It's Didi." Sunny crossed her arms and glared at the wall. It was going to be a long ride to Vienna.

10:08

"So, we've been talking about genes and inheritance of traits from parents," the science teacher said, looking at the rows of faces from Class 8F. "Who can give me an example of inherited characteristics?"

A half-dozen hands went up.

"Yes?" the teacher said, and pointed.

"Curly hair," said a girl at the front.

"Yes, very good. The curliness of hair depends on how flat the individual strands are. Ribbon-like ones curl up while round ones do not." She pointed again.

"Red hair, miss," offered a boy at the back.

"Correct. A lot of colouration is genetically controlled, like hair colour, eye colour, skin colour, even how much you can tan."

"Goofy teeth," blurted out the class clown to a chorus of giggles.

"We don't call it that, but yes, dental overcrowding is also genetic." The teacher's eyes scanned the room for anyone who might not be paying attention and landed on

Donna, who was staring out of the window.

"Donna!" the teacher called.

"Hm?" Donna blinked and looked up, startled.

"Can you please give the class an example of genetic inheritance and why it might be useful to know?"

Sam and Arun, sitting behind Donna, exchanged looks of concern.

Donna straightened up. "All right, miss. My cousin, Lateesha – she's sixteen, right? – got pregnant by this boy Marlon and, when she said to him, it's your kid so you gotta pay for it, he was like, 'No way, I see you hangin' with this other guy, Jerome, so how do I know he's not the daddy? Make him pay.' You with me?"

The teacher stared, open-mouthed, and nodded.

Donna resumed. "Now, Lateesha's real smart, so she punches Marlon in the mouth, busts his lip and makes him bleed. She then did the same thing to the other guy, Jerome, only she popped his nose. And when they both wiped up their blood, she kept the tissues. Nine months later, when the baby was born, she did a check on all the blood types and the baby was Type B. Lateesha is Type O and so is Jerome, but Marlon is Type AB, so he had to be the father. They're married now, so it's good."

The teacher opened and closed her mouth, gaping like

a fish, before she was able to say, "That's ... excellent. Yes, blood types are genetic. I would have thought knowing it for transfusions was a simpler example, but yes, very good."

Donna turned round in her chair to face Arun and Sam and whispered, "Did you see her face? I totally just made that up."

High in the Austrian Alps, to the east of Innsbruck, the nine-car armoured train snaked its way along the track cut into the majestic mountains. Sheer cliffs pressed in on all sides with steep, towering faces.

Lying flat on his front and scanning the snowy vista through a pair of high-powered binoculars, Dusan swept his view westwards, past the throngs of skiers below, beyond the bustling ski lodges and chalet hotels of the nearby resort, and came to rest on the rolling gunmetal-grey train carriages, heading east. The lookout reached for his walkie-talkie.

"Alpha team? Status report," Dusan said.

"Alpha team leader here. All armed and ready," came the reply.

"The package is on its way. I repeat, the package is on its way. As soon as the train reaches the tunnel, I'll give you the signal. You know what to do."

On board the train, Moss was perched on his seat, peering into the aisle, looking up and down the train.

"Can't you just sit still?" Sunny snapped. "Read a book, if you still remember how."

Moss ignored the jibe. "Don't you want to know what's on this train?"

"There might be nothing," Sunny said. "This could just be a training exercise for us all. Our brief was to watch and learn from the professionals. That's what Mr Quinn is measuring us on."

Moss rolled his eyes. "Come on, Sunny. You don't really believe that. I've known you too long. This is far too elaborate for a training gig. There's definitely something important on this train."

Sunny lowered the magazine she was reading. "All right, I admit I am curious, but Mr Quinn told us to lay low."

"Quinn's a spy. That's what he's recruiting us for. He'd want us to find out what the train is carrying. And how do you know that's not what he really wants us to do? Maybe that's our real mission."

"OK, but we'll have to be careful, in case we aren't supposed to snoop around. That way, we can play dumb if we need to."

"Agreed. I'm good at that. We have three teams of Austrian Jagdkommando Special Forces on board, plus a dozen police. That's a lot of firepower. Question is, why?"

Outside, the train slowed as it rounded a wide curve and was swallowed by the shadow of surrounding peaks. It glided past a ski resort on the northern slopes and approached the mouth of a tunnel, carved deep into a mountain.

Dusan kept his binoculars fixed on the train and waited for the moment it entered the tunnel.

"Now!" he said into the radio.

KABOOM!

Five kilometres away, at the far end of the Kallstein railway tunnel, a series of explosions punched its way high across the cliff face, blasting tonnes of gneiss and slate into the sky. Thunderous echoes reverberated around the adjacent cliffs and a black cloud of debris soared aloft before raining down.

KRAKKK!

From deep within the rock face, a split widened into a lateral crack and an immense stone slab sheared off and crashed down on to the rail tracks below, sealing the eastern end of the tunnel ahead of the onrushing train.

10:17

Inside the train, Moss stood in the aisle, trying to see past the Austrian operatives and into the centrally located cargo truck.

"All you're going to see is a locked door. That's how it works when they don't want you to know," Sunny said, looking up from her magazine. "We should wait until someone goes in and maybe we can see something over their shoulder."

"What if I see them punch a code into a keypad or something? Might be useful for— *WAAAAAAAGGGHHH!*"

Three things happened at once: the lights went out, plunging the carriage into complete blackness; an ear-splitting alarm sounded, drowning out all other noise; and the train's pneumatic brakes locked hard, killing its speed.

SKREEEEEEEEEEE!

Unfortunately, the train slowed down but its passengers didn't. Forward momentum flung Sunny out of her seat to bounce off the opposite recliner. Moss wasn't as lucky and took off down the aisle, slamming into a dividing wall, while flight cases tumbled from overhead racks.

Corporal Mertens, reacting quickly, sprang to his feet and tapped an illuminated control pad on the wall. The alarm stopped and red emergency lighting blinked on.

Moss got to his knees and was promptly thrown over again by the sudden lurch of the train finally coming to a stop.

"Is anyone hurt?" Mertens asked.

"No, all good here," Moss said, his fingers feeling the fresh dent in the chest of his body armour.

"What the heck happened?" Sunny said, climbing into the aisle. "This is not a scheduled stop."

Mertens returned to the wall pad and activated the train intercom to speak to the driver. After a rapid exchange in German, he turned and said, "There's been a rockfall ahead. The tunnel is completely blocked. We're lucky the driver was able to stop in time."

"A rockfall?" Moss said. "Does that happen often?"

"No, hardly ever, which makes me very suspicious."

Mertens gave an order to his team and the commandos gathered the flight cases, opened them and began retrieving the weapons stored inside. The click and snap of loading ammunition clips filled the air.

Moss nodded to Sunny. "Do you think I should ask if we can borrow some?" he said.

"I'm sure they'll be delighted to hand us their guns, just like that," Sunny said.

"My dad always said, don't ask, don't get." Moss shuffled over to Corporal Friedrich. "Um, Petra, I was, uh, wondering, if you have some spare sidearms, would you mind letting us—"

Friedrich smiled and leaned over, close enough to touch noses. "Yes, I do mind," she said, "so the answer is no."

She raised her hand and signalled for her team to spread out across the carriage.

Moss slunk back to Sunny, who was choking back a laugh. "That was cold," she said. "Nice to see you haven't lost your famous way with women."

Moss scowled in reply. "Maybe you should have asked Dodo." He held up his wristwatch and tapped the face. "Do you think it's time for this?"

Sunny's smile vanished. "Will it even work? Radio waves don't travel underground."

"It depends how far into the tunnel we are. I'm guessing the end we came in from is clear."

"Mr Quinn said emergency use only."

Moss pointed at the six Special Forces soldiers, armed and guarding the entry points to the carriage. "Surely this counts as an emergency?" he said.

The red emergency lighting blinked out, leaving the room in total darkness, apart from the green glow of Moss's watch.

"It does now," Sunny said.

Corporal Mertens swore, switched on his flashlight and went for the illuminated intercom pad.

"What's wrong?" Moss asked him.

"Emergency lights are fed by battery. There's no way they would go out but leave the comms working, unless their circuit was cut."

"Cut? By who?"

Mertens spoke to the driver: "*Können Sie den Zug umkehren?*"

"*Ja, verstanden,*" the driver replied. "*Bereitstehen.*"

"What was that about?" Moss asked.

"You'll see," Mertens said.

With a deafening hiss, which sounded even louder within the confines of the rail tunnel, the air brakes released and the train began to roll slowly, reversing back towards the open end of the tunnel.

* * *

Still watching, through binoculars trained on the tunnel entrance and walkie-talkie in hand, Dusan pressed the call button.

"They are coming back, as predicted," he said. "Alpha team, you know what to do."

Picking up speed, the reversing train clattered towards the ever-growing circle of daylight at the mouth of the tunnel.

To the north, directly above the railway tracks, another exciting day of winter sports was underway at the Kallstein resort. Holidaymakers of all ages vacated their chalets and hotels to join snowboarders and skiers on the freshly prepared slopes, while cafes and restaurants were busy serving late breakfasts. A string of cable cars ferried passengers up the slopes to the top end of the ski runs. No one had heard the previous explosions, five kilometres away with a mountain in between.

BA-DOOMMM!

The air shook again under the detonation of a second set of mining explosives, placed high above the mouth of the open train tunnel below the slopes. Skiers stopped at the unexpected roar of thunder and watched a black cloud of rock dust engulf the rocky mountainside. Surprise turned to horror as a cascade of boulders rumbled down to seal the western tunnel entrance beneath them.

10:31

Back at Secret Intelligence headquarters, Quinn marched into the busy Communications Hub and zeroed in on a technician listening intently on her headphones.

"Yes?" he said.

"GCHQ picked up a partial message," the technician said. "It was an SOS signal, encrypted and on one of our frequencies."

"From whom?" Quinn said.

"We're trying to confirm the trace from the equipment ID, but it was issued to you last year. That's why I called you."

Quinn softened and lowered his voice. "Do you know where that signal was sent from?"

"It's not easy to get a lock because it was quite broken up and it cut off halfway." The technician tapped her keyboard, calling up detailed maps.

"Give me a ball park. Which continent?"

"The signal was sent from the Austrian Alps. I know that because the nearest receiving station was Innsbruck."

Quinn swore. "Low-frequency pulse? Came through in bits?"

The technician nodded.

"Run me a scan on mobile phone traffic in the area. Anywhere that's had a sudden spike in call volume."

"That would be here." She tapped the screen at a mountainous valley. "There's a ski resort nearby. Emergency services have also gone mad."

"Can you get me a live satellite feed? Zoom in on the railway?"

The technician took off her headphones. "I'm going to need authorisation for that. I can't just—"

Quinn straightened up. "Who's in charge here?" he yelled.

Other technicians shrank at their listening stations and cupped their hands over their headphones.

"*Shhhhh!*" hissed the duty manager, hurrying over. "We're trying to work here."

"And you'll be working somewhere else if you don't make yourself useful," Quinn barked.

"I won't be spoken to this way," said the manager. "Please leave."

"I don't have time for this," Quinn said, grabbing the manager by the tie. He tightened his grip and twisted the knot.

"Urk," gurgled the manager.

Quinn turned to the technician. "What do you need? Swipe card? Thumbprint? Eyeball?"

"Swipe card will do," she said, and gave a weak smile.

"Fine." Quinn snapped the lanyard dangling from his captive's neck and handed over the card. He released his chokehold on the manager, who stumbled away in search of a security guard.

The technician pressed the card against a reader and logged on to the orbital feed. "Satellite view coming into focus now..." she said. "Tracking along the railway. Oh. There's been a landslide."

"Let me see that." Quinn watched over the analyst's shoulder as she zoomed in on the resort side of the Kallstein railway tunnel. "Show me the other end of the tunnel," he said.

The analyst slid the picture to view the eastern mouth of the tunnel. Here, too, a jumble of tiny grains and pebbles were scattered over the train tracks.

"A landslide at both ends?" Quinn said. "That's no accident."

"Why have we stopped? Are we outside the tunnel,

already?" Moss asked the tall Austrian soldier. "That was quick."

"Too quick." Mertens spoke to the driver again over the intercom, before reporting, "There's been another rockfall, this time on the western side. Both ends of the tunnel are sealed."

"That can't be right," Sunny said. "What happened, an earthquake?"

THUMP-THUMP-THUMP-THUMP came from overhead.

A beam of light from Corporal Friedrich's torch followed the sound. "*Schritte*," she said, taking aim at the ceiling with her Steyr sub-machine gun.

"There's someone on the roof?" Moss said. "Great. Hey, you!" he yelled. "Help! We're trapped in here! *Mnmmff!*"

"Quiet!" Friedrich snapped, keeping her gloved hand over Moss's mouth. "It's dark, we have no power and we're stuck inside this train. Haven't you thought that it might be those outside who have done this?"

"Everyone, hold your positions," Mertens said to his fellow commandos. "Cover all exits and entrances. No one's coming in."

Moss peeled Friedrich's hand off his mouth and ducked down beside Sunny.

"I've got a better idea," Sunny whispered to Moss. "We

should try getting out."

"But all the doors are locked," he said.

"What about windows?"

"There aren't any. It's an armoured train."

Sunny thought about it for a moment before saying loudly, "I'm going to be sick. I need the toilet."

10:42

"He's in a meeting, you can't go in," protested the secretary, but Quinn ignored him, shoved open the heavy oak door and strode into the office of "C", the Chief of British Intelligence.

C was speaking on the telephone with his back to the door. He rotated his chair, caught the look on Quinn's face and said, "I'll have to call you back, Prime Minister." He ended the call. "Anyone else I'd have shot for that," he said to Quinn.

"I'm flattered, sir, but I don't have time for pleasantries." Quinn rested both palms on C's desk. "I have two agents in serious trouble."

"How serious?"

"On a scale of ten? Eleven."

C removed his half-moon spectacles and folded them. "You're not one to exaggerate. Who are they?"

"You don't know them. It's an off-the-books operation. I needed someone I can trust so I went outside the Service."

C took a deep breath, held it and exhaled. "You know I

don't condone any black ops missions."

"It's not like that, sir. It's all above board. These are potential new recruits. I sent them on a watching brief only. They don't even know why they're there or what they're watching."

"And where, exactly, is 'there'?"

"Currently, a freight train, trapped in a tunnel in the Austrian Alps. Someone stopped that train, deliberately, by blowing up both ends of the tunnel."

C leaned back in his chair. "Tell me more."

"Last month, one of my snouts overheard something about a possible plan to hijack this train. It didn't sound feasible, but I put these two noobs on board, just in case."

"What's so special about the cargo which makes it worth stealing?"

Quinn leaned forward, took a pen from C's desk and scribbled a few words on the nearest piece of blank paper. C glanced at the note and raised an eyebrow.

"I can see why you didn't want anyone to know," he said. "Not after last time. Why did you think it wasn't feasible?"

"Sir, it's an armoured train, doing a hundred kilometres an hour, guarded by three squads of Austrian Special Forces soldiers and a dozen armed police…"

C chewed his lower lip. "What's the worst-case

scenario here?"

"With those Jagdkommando teams on board, there'll be no messing around. If it all kicks off, we're talking ketchup everywhere, a total bloodbath."

"Which will be difficult to explain. Do we have any assets in the area?"

"No. We'd never get anyone there in time and, if we did, how are they going to get through a hundred tonnes of rock?"

C stood up, walked over to a side table and poured a large whisky.

"Not for me, please, sir," Quinn said. "I need a clear head."

"I didn't pour it for you," C said, taking a gulp. "What's your play, Quinn? You came here for approval, not for advice."

"I don't think we have much choice, sir. I want to activate the *S.T.E.A.L.T.H.* initiative."

Anger flashed in C's eyes. "Out of the question! This is the worst possible time, what with the defence select committee sniffing around. You know how hard we've worked to bury the truth about its existence. And now you want the darned thing to pop up in the Alps?"

"All right, sir," Quinn said. "If I can't get your approval, I'll take your advice. Do you have a better idea to get our people out from under a hundred tonnes of rock and to safeguard the cargo if it all goes pear-shaped?"

C closed his eyes and lowered his head. Quinn wasn't sure if his chief was thinking or praying.

"I don't like it," C said at last, locking eyes with Quinn, "not one bit, but I'll go with it, on two conditions. One, *S.T.E.A.L.T.H.* stays out of sight, effectively invisible. Two, this conversation never took place."

"Thank you, sir," Quinn said. "I've already set the wheels in motion." He started to move towards the door.

"And Quinn?"

Quinn stopped in his tracks.

"Just so you know, if this mission goes south, I will burn you and your whole operation down to the ground. There will be no coming back for you."

"Understood, sir."

Back in science class at the Most Sacred Heart High School, the teacher was pressing on with the lesson.

"And, speaking of selective breeding, who can tell me what broccoli, cauliflower, cabbage, kale and Brussels sprouts all have in common?" she asked.

"No one likes 'em, miss," came a voice from the back.

TAP-TAP. The door swung open and the headmaster

came in, brandishing a printout. With a rasping of chairs, the pupils all stood. The class teacher motioned for them to sit again.

"This is 8F, yes?" asked the flustered-looking headteacher. "I need Arun Lal, Donna Critchlow and Sam Evans, please. Can you collect your things and come with me? Hurry, hurry."

Class members looked at each other, perplexed, while the three named pupils trudged to the front.

"Follow me, please," said the head, and led them out into the corridor.

"What's going on, sir?" Arun asked.

"Have we done something wrong?" Donna said.

"No, it's nothing like that." The headmaster stopped, gathered the children into a huddle and skimmed the email in his hand. "You three are required at an inter-school sports event, starting at eleven o'clock."

"You what?" Sam said in disbelief. "Me?"

"You were randomly selected, apparently. It's all very strange. I can swear there was nothing about this in my inbox or calendar but then I got a phone call asking where you were and there it all was, with email thread, parental permission, acknowledgements, all going back days, so I must have dropped the ball somehow. I'm terribly sorry."

"That's OK, sir, you've probably been working too hard," Donna said. "We were starting to think they'd cancelled it or something when no one came for us." She winked at Arun.

"We were?" Sam said.

"Yeah, I've been looking forward to this all week," Arun said, warming to the story. "I even got some training in."

"I'm glad you're so keen," the headmaster said. "They sent a car for you, because you're late. It's waiting in front. Do your best. You're representing the honour of the school. Remember, it's not winning that matters, it's taking part."

"Said like a true loser," Donna muttered under her breath.

10:53

The stalled train sat silently at the western end of the Kallstein railway tunnel, its gunmetal-grey shell glowing beneath the recessed lighting. Thick cables snaked along the tunnel walls and ceiling, carrying power, signalling and communications.

Dark shapes flitted among the shadows and clambered on top of the carriages.

Crouching down beside a roof-mounted ventilation unit, one of the intruders levered a crowbar to prise off the covering panel. Four high-powered fans whirred, two drawing external air into the carriage and two extracting air outwards. A second figure, wearing a gas mask, set down a heavy tank of compressed gas, clipped a hose to the nozzle and opened the valve. A jet of white mist hissed from the end of the hose and the masked figure directed it down towards the spinning intake fans.

Inside the train, Sunny had found a toilet cubicle. She stood in the half-open doorway watching from the light of her phone torch while Moss bounced from one wall to the other, kicking savagely at the steel casing.

"No!" Moss yelled, stopping to punch the wall. "How can there be no windows in a toilet, of all places? That's disgusting."

"It was worth a try," Sunny said. "I know high-speed trains don't have opening windows, to stop idiots chucking things out, but as this is a freight train…"

"Ugh." Moss aimed a kick below the wash basin, buckling the panel.

"I don't think vandalising the toilet is going to help us much."

"You're not helping me here, Sunny. I'm trying to find a way out and all you can do is criticise."

THUD!

Sunny spun in the direction of the sound – *THUD!* – and saw a second commando slump to the floor.

"Gas!" shouted Corporal Mertens, still on his feet. He took a deep breath, held it and dived for the gas mask in his equipment case.

Sunny jumped into the toilet and slammed the door behind her. "Some kind of knockout gas," she said, eyes wide with alarm. "Will we be safe in here?"

"No, we won't," Moss said, pointing at a ventilation grille

in the door.

Sunny grabbed a handful of paper towels and knelt to try and stuff them into the grille.

"Wait, I may have an idea." Moss looked at the toilet. "Good thing this is an older train."

Returning to the smashed panel beneath the sink, he pulled aside the steel cover and reached in to yank at a mesh-covered hose, pulling it loose from the tap. He ripped the other end free, went to the toilet and stepped on the floor-mounted flush. Clean water from an internal tank swirled and a flap valve opened to release the liquid on to the tracks below. Moss jabbed one end of the hose through the open flap. The other end he held to his mouth.

"No," Sunny said. "There's no way I'm putting that in my mouth."

"Trust me," Moss said. "This is a drop chute toilet. Everything goes out of the train and on to the tracks."

"That's revolting!"

"True, but it means we have an air supply from the outside. Watch." He wiped the end of the tubing with a paper towel, put his mouth over it and sucked in a lungful of air, which he held. He waved the hose at Sunny.

"Sometimes I hate this job," she muttered, and took the tube.

41

"I knew it!" Donna said in triumph, when she saw the black Range Rover waiting in the school car park. "Who else could've pulled that stunt?"

"So, we finally get a call," Arun said. "Took long enough."

"I don't like it," Sam said. "It's got to be really bad if MI6 are calling us."

"Get in!" Burgess called from the window. "Old Spice will explain on the way."

"Who's that?" Donna said.

"Must be one of Mr Quinn's new boys," Arun said. "The last lot all got binned."

The kids climbed into the back of the Range Rover and Burgess sped out of the school gates.

"There's an iPad in the pocket," Burgess said, eyeing the pupils in his rear-view mirror. "Just tap the screen."

Arun took the tablet computer from the seat pouch and switched it on. Quinn's face loomed from the screen.

"Hello, children," he said.

Donna, Sam and Arun all looked at each other.

"That wasn't at all creepy," Donna said. "What is this, nursery school?"

"Fine. Hello, you pre-pubescent pains in my rear."

"Much better!" Donna laughed. "So, what is it you

42

want, old man?"

Burgess raised an eyebrow and continued to watch the children through the mirror.

"Let's stick to code names for now, Posh."

"Yeah, about that. I want to change mine."

"Me, too," Arun said. "I don't think Ginger suits me."

"Forget that!" Quinn said. "Fill in a form later and pick a new one. Right now, I have a job for you."

"Do we get paid?" Donna asked.

"Of course you don't get paid. That was never the deal. You don't go to jail, either, remember? Or you can go back to class. Burge, turn the car around."

"No!" Arun said. "We'll hear you out."

"I'm happy to go back," Sam said.

Quinn glared back from the screen. "I have two agents trapped on a train in a tunnel under the Austrian Alps. A landslide at each end has blocked them in. I want you three to use You Know What to bring those agents home."

"How can one landslide block two ends of a tunnel?" Arun said.

"It's two landslides, one at either end."

"How is that possible? I mean, there's, like, a mountain in the middle."

"Who cares how it's possible? That's what's happened.

Now, are you up for the task or not?"

"This train," Donna said. "There are other people on board, right, not just your two agents? What do we do with them?"

"I'm making it really simple," Quinn said. "Fly in, extract my two agents, fly out. That's it. Nothing else. Understand?"

"But MANDROID was built for search and rescue," Arun protested. "We might be able to get the whole train out and help everyone."

"That's Austria's problem. Let them deal with it. I just want my agents back."

"All right," Arun said. "Although that does sound pretty selfish."

"Good. Burge has the coordinates for you. And one more thing."

"Yes?"

"Don't be seen. I want you invisible. No pictures, no selfies, no TV, nothing. Don't go posting snaps on Instagram."

"Wait!" Donna said, looking alarmed. "Did you say 'Alps'? Will there be snow?"

"And they wonder why I hate kids," Quinn muttered, as he ended the call.

11:01

Huddled beside the train toilet, using Sunny's phone as a torch, Moss took a deep breath from the mesh-covered tubing and passed it to Sunny to do the same. After holding his breath for a minute, Moss exhaled the spent air and took another draw from the hose.

Sunny checked her phone battery and saw it was low.

Suddenly, the sound of combat boots clumped past the door and a voice said, "*Schnell! Die Ladung schützen.*"

"That was one of our guys," Sunny said. "Do you think the gas has cleared?"

Moss looked at this watch. "Maybe. It takes a couple of minutes to completely vent the air in a carriage. If we have people running around and shouting, it should be OK."

"I wish I'd studied German when I was in school."

"Me, too. Whoever it was, they were heading towards the front of the train."

"Towards the cargo truck?"

Moss nodded. "You thinking what I'm thinking?"

"I've been working with you too long. Yep, let's go."

Sunny eased the toilet door open and peered out. Her phone torch picked out four Special Forces commandos slumped across the floor.

"Looks like the coast is clear," she said to Moss.

THUMP-THUMP-THUMP. Footsteps sounded on the roof again.

"We'd better get a move on," Moss said. He knelt to take two flashlights, a pair of Glock automatic pistols and a P90 sub-machine gun from the unconscious commandos.

Outside the train, in the illuminated tunnel, a tall, stocky individual watched his various teams at work. He stood with his legs wide apart, back straight and arms folded. On his head was a round cloth hat with a V-shaped indent running from front to back.

"Prepare to move in," he growled.

An explosives expert climbed up on to the running board beneath one of the train doors and pressed C-4 charges against the lock and hinges. He inserted wired detonators and jumped down again.

"Clear!" he called, and waited for the other troops to take cover. Once everyone was hunkered down, he triggered the explosives.

BOOM!

The door crumpled like tin foil and dropped from its

frame, clanging on to the tunnel floor, a twisted wreck of smoking scrap.

The waiting strike team adjusted their night-vision goggles, switched on the laser sights mounted to their assault rifles and headed for the open doorway.

Burgess parked the black Range Rover outside Evans Builder's Yard and got out to open the door for Sam, Arun and Donna. He handed Sam a flash drive and went to the back of the car where he reached in for a large rucksack that still had the store labels hanging from it.

"Here you go," he said to Arun, presenting him with the rucksack. "And good luck, you lot. I've seen what you can do." He winked and returned to the car.

"That was weird," Sam said as they walked into his dad's yard. "Have we met that bloke before?"

"Uh-uh," Donna said. "Although..."

"This thing weighs a ton," Arun grumbled, struggling under the weight of the rucksack.

"Ooh, you think there are guns in there?" Donna said, prodding the pack. "Guns are heavy."

"No!" Sam replied. "That's not what this is. It's a simple rescue. Don't get any ideas."

"Someone's moody," Donna observed.

"Am not!"

They stopped beside a large, tarpaulin-covered structure, about the size and shape of a shipping container.

"It's been a while," Arun said, setting down the pack. "How's he been?"

"I've been keeping him company," Sam answered. "Learning more about what he can do."

He went round and loosened the clasps on the straps holding the tarpaulin in place, before pulling it free to reveal a large, multi-wheeled motor home, resplendent in blue and gold.

Donna went straight for the door, only for Sam to throw himself in the gap.

"Maybe I should go in first," he said.

Donna gave him a withering look. "Excuse me," she said. "If it wasn't for me, you'd still be waiting outside for someone to let you in."

"No, please don't—"

It was too late. Donna pulled open the door, mounted the step and yelled, "Seriously?"

Arun saw the terrified look on Sam's face. "I'll try and calm her down," he said, climbing up after her.

The interior was as he remembered it, with a long

gangway and three thick, padded chairs, each encircled by an array of instrument panels. What he didn't remember was the assortment of snack-food wrappers, plastic bottles, cartons and empty drink cans that littered the floor.

"How much time has he spent in here?" Donna said. "It looks like his bedroom."

Arun turned in the doorway. "Sam, get a bin bag, and hurry." Sam scurried away, his face burning scarlet.

Donna shook her head. "Why do you put up with him?" she asked Arun. "You're not like that."

Arun shrugged. "Sam's just Sam. It's how he is. It doesn't make him a bad person or anything. We're all different."

"Some more than others," Donna said. "Still, how are we supposed to work in this?"

A black bin bag appeared in the doorway, waving like a flag of surrender. "I'll clean it," Sam said.

"You'd better," Donna added.

"We'll all do it," Arun said firmly, kneeling to scoop up some crisp packets.

11:09

"Did you hear that?" Moss whispered, and switched off his torch. Hunched low in the pitch black of the train interior, he looked back towards the rear of the train. Faint pools of light bobbed in the distance.

"They're inside the train," Sunny breathed from beside him. "Sweeping each carriage."

"And coming this way." Moss fished a grubby handkerchief from his pocket, wrapped it around the flashlight and turned it back on. The muted glow was just enough to determine the outlines of the passageway.

They both crept silently along the floor, on hands and knees, towards the doorway to the next carriage. Moss reached up for the handle, unlatched it and slowly swung the door open, praying it had been well oiled and wouldn't creak.

As soon as the door opened, the cold muzzle of a gun jabbed against his throat and a gloved hand covered his mouth.

* * *

"So why isn't he talking to us?" Donna said, waving her hand to indicate her surroundings. "Last time he wouldn't shut up."

"I put him into power-saving mode," Sam said, squeezing a Pringles tube into the overflowing bin bag. "Shall I wake him up?"

"Well, we're not going to get very far otherwise. I'm pretty sure Quinny didn't want us to walk the whole way."

"Oh, gosh. This is so embarrassing," Sam said. He clapped his hands twice and shouted, "Ahoy, matey!"

Ahoy, Captain Evans! said the flat computer voice. *Are we ready to set sail?*

"What the actual heck?" Donna demanded.

Sam's cheeks flushed scarlet. "Uh, well ... it started out as kind of a game, playing pirates, and it, um, got out of hand," he stammered.

"I'll say!"

Arun leaned on the arm of the nearest seat. "Sam, what happened?" he said gently.

"Well, you know how Andy kept—"

"Andy?" Donna cut in.

"It's what I call him, short for MANDROID. I couldn't call him 'Mandy', so I dropped the M. Anyhow, so Andy kept calling you Commander Lal, right, after your dad, so I thought what's higher than Commander and it's a Captain, in the navy, so I got him to start calling me Captain and it, uh, went from there."

Arun blinked at Sam a few times before deciding against pursuing this line of thought.

"MANDROID," he said. "System report?"

Aye, Commander. All systems are online and operating at full power. Arrr! The ship is ready to sail.

"OK," Arun said. "Let's ditch the rubbish, see what's in the rucksack and get moving."

"You're lucky I don't throw you out," Donna muttered at Sam as he trudged past with the bin bag.

Arun put his head in his hands. Maybe being in school wasn't so bad after all.

Shifting his weight on to his knees, Moss raised both hands in surrender.

"The Englishman?" a voice said in surprise. Moss felt the gun muzzle leave his neck and he returned to all fours.

Corporal Mertens stared at him in disbelief. "And the *fräulein*. How are you still moving?"

Sunny crawled alongside. "Can we get out of this doorway and away from those armed men and then discuss this?"

"Yes, of course. You're right. Come with me."

Mertens waited for the two ex-police officers to join him in the vestibule between train cars and closed the door.

"Stay low," he instructed, and led the way into the next carriage, using his torch for light. They passed another five unconscious commandos before coming to a heavy security door at the end. Mertens punched a 10-digit sequence into the keypad and the lock disengaged with a heavy clunk.

He heaved the door open and led the way into the freight wagon, a heavily armoured carriage with an LED lantern hanging from the ceiling and eight large crates stacked on pallets in the middle.

Three other Jagdkommando officers were positioned behind the crates, their Steyr AUG assault rifles trained on the door.

Moss recognised Corporal Friedrich, who lowered her weapon when she saw him. "*Unglaublich*," she said.

Mertens resealed the door and beckoned his teammates forward.

"Look who I found," he said. "Our English friends somehow avoided the gas."

"How?" Friedrich asked, her voice heavy with suspicion.

"You don't have this." She held up her gas mask.

"No, but I have this," Moss said, tapping his temple.

"Now isn't the time for being obtuse," Sunny said. "We were in the toilet. The flush empties outside so we were able to get some clean air that way, from below the train."

The other two commandos nodded in approval.

"These are Corporals Buhringer and Schäplitz," Mertens said, indicating each in turn. Buhringer was bald with a round face and Schäplitz sported a trim moustache and a buzz cut. "No one else made it."

"So it's six of us versus how many of them?"

"We don't know, but I suspect we are going to find out very soon."

11:16

Sam returned from disposing of the rubbish. "What's in the rucksack?" he asked.

Arun unzipped it, reached inside and hauled out a heavy winter jacket with a fur-trimmed hood and a new label hanging from it. "Looks like there's three coats and three sets of ski pants," he said.

"I don't do cold," Donna said, crossing her arms and leaning back against a console.

"I'm sorry?" Arun said.

"Read my lips. I. Don't. Do. Cold. Or snow." She sucked her teeth.

"What does that even mean?" Sam said.

"Yes, you do," Arun challenged Donna. "You've come to school in winter."

"That's different. I got a lift. Look at me, Arun, do I look like I'm meant for a cold climate?"

"Half of you is," Sam said.

"Excuse me?"

"Your dad's English half. That half can deal with cold."

Sam looked to Arun for support. "Right?"

"I'm not so sure about that," Arun said. "I think body size and fat play a part, too, not just genes. You're on thin ice there."

Donna was speechless, but not for long. "Fine," she said, "but I am *not* going out into any snow so you can put that stuff right back in the bag. Got it?"

"Loud and clear," Arun said, punching the coat back into the rucksack.

Sam rooted around in his pocket for the flash drive Burgess had given him. "Let's see where we're going," he said. He found a USB slot on the cockpit display and slotted home the memory stick. "MANDROID, full holographic display, please."

Aye, Captain. Is it a treasure map you're seeking?

"That pirate talk has to stop," Donna said under her breath.

A deck of holographic slides, each a metre wide, flashed into the air above the console. Sam brushed them with his fingers, flipping through the set. Customised maps showing contours, terrain, topography, thermal imaging, climate, transport links, all whizzed past.

"Here we are." Sam stopped at a satellite photo showing a snow-covered mountainside. It was centred on two accumulations of rock, and a dotted line linking them snaked through the cliff face. He widened his hands to enlarge the zoom on the picture.

"Where is this?" Arun asked.

"The Kallstein railway tunnel, near to a place called Bad Häring," Sam read out. "The train went in, headed east, and a landslide blocked the far end. When the train tried to reverse out, a second, smaller landslide blocked the tracks at the western end."

"Trapping them inside," Arun said. "That has to be deliberate. Why?"

"Someone must really have a thing for trains to go to that much trouble," Donna said.

Captain Evans, I have an incoming message, arr! said MANDROID

"Put it on screen," Sam said.

Quinn's angry face flickered into view on the head-up display. "*S.T.E.A.L.T.H.* team, are you en route yet?" he said. "Do you have an ETA?"

Sam looked around for help.

"Don't ask me," Arun said. "You're the Captain, so you outrank me."

"Uh, that's a negative, Old Spice," Sam said to Quinn, using the code name the kids had chosen for him. "We were checking through the coats and looking at the map. Cool satellite pictures, though."

Quinn tried not to explode. "Next time, get yourselves moving and *then* look at the goodies and pretty pictures. Do you think you can manage that for me?"

"Yeah, I suppose," Sam said.

"Then get going!" Quinn ended the call.

"MANDROID, pre-flight check," Arun said.

All systems shipshape and ready to set sail.

"Hold on!" Donna said. "We can't just lift off here in the middle of town. There's too many people. We have to go somewhere less noticeable."

"You're right," Arun said. "We're not meant to be seen."

"How about Richmond Park?" Sam said. "We can cut through, go off road and then use some trees for cover."

"Sounds good to me," Arun said. "Let's go."

Moments later, the gleaming motor home pulled out of the builder's yard, in self-driving mode, and turned south. It may have looked like a motorised caravan but, with its ability to reconfigure its components down to the microscopic level, that was just one of many vehicles it could change into.

Ruby-coloured beams of light swept across the interior

of the train carriage, gliding over passenger seats and slumped commandos, criss-crossing in a vivid web. The strike team spread out, their night-vision goggles and gas masks making them look like some strange species of humanoid insect.

The point man paused by a toilet door and raised his fist as a signal to stop. He pushed the door open with the muzzle of his gun and noted the broken panel beneath the sink, the metal hose on the floor and the raised toilet lid.

Backing out, he resumed the sweep of carriages before coming to the heavy steel door of the freight wagon.

"Major? We're here," he said into his walkie-talkie. "It's all clean, exactly as planned."

"I'll be right there," came the reply.

"I can hear someone out there, just about," Sunny said. She had her ear pressed to the cold metal surface of the freight wagon door.

"You must have very good hearing," Friedrich said.

"Can they get in?" Moss said, looking to his Austrian compatriots.

"It won't be easy," said Schäplitz, the engineering specialist. He stroked his moustache while he was thinking.

"The locks and hinges are all behind steel plate so they won't be able to cut through or blast it easily."

"Besides," added Buhringer, the team's communications specialist, "any explosive would do as much damage on their side. To use enough to blow through the door would destroy the cargo, too, and then it's no good to them." His bald head gleamed under the LED lamp.

"I'm not convinced," Moss said. "If they're clever enough to stop the train, take out most of the guards and isolate this wagon, they must have a way to get in."

"Or do they wait for us to come out?" Sunny said. "Aren't we going to use up all the air in here, with six of us breathing?"

"Fortunately, this isn't an airtight container," Mertens said. "There's ventilation but not where they can access it. We're safe in here for now."

Moss pulled a sour expression. "I've heard that one before and let's just say it didn't go well."

11:22

One of the distinctive things about the London Borough of Richmond upon Thames is that about half of the area is parkland. As well as Hampton Court and Kew Gardens, the borough is also home to Richmond Park, the largest of London's Royal Parks at 2,360 acres.

Heading south down Richmond Hill, the blue and gold camper van squeezed between the narrow pillars of Richmond Gate and into the leafy expanse beyond.

"MANDROID, maintain speed at twenty miles per hour, max, and start scanning for any areas that are empty of people and cars," Arun said, sitting in the cockpit seat.

Behind him, in the mid-section, Donna said, "And no more of that pirate stuff, OK? Whatever weird games you play with Sam is strictly between the two of you. I'm not part of it, you hear?"

Aye-aye, Petty Officer Critchlow, said MANDROID.

"Whoa!" Donna said. "Petty Officer?"

Sam, sitting in the back, shrank into his seat.

"Is that higher or lower than Captain or Commander?"

Donna continued.

"MANDROID, you don't have to answer that," Arun said, trying to head off trouble.

Petty Officer is the lowest of the senior ratings.

"Is that so?" Donna swivelled her seat to glower at Sam, whose cheeks were flushed. "What's the highest rank?" she asked him.

"Admiral," Sam squeaked.

"That's it, then," Donna declared. "I'm an Admiral."

"I thought you weren't doing the pirate thing."

The vehicle followed Sawyer's Hill Road eastward, through the park, past rolling meadows, clumps of woodland and a roaming herd of deer. It came to a mini roundabout.

"Take the right turn," Arun said. "It's marked for authorised vehicles only, so it should be quieter."

"But we're not an authorised vehicle," Sam protested.

"First they got to find us, then they got to catch us," Donna said. "Go for it, MANDROID. Admiral's orders."

The motor home executed a sharp turn and crept along the narrow road, which bisected a wide tract of grass before reaching a wooded area.

"This is good," Arun said. "MANDROID, make a turn off the road and on to the grass. Find some trees for cover and prepare for vertical take-off."

In the tunnel, a black-clad operative snapped a salute at the brooding figure with the V-shaped hat. "Major, everything is in position. The train is secured."

"You've counted the prisoners?"

"Yes, sir. All of the train crew, police and commandos have been restrained and locked into the passenger car. Only four are unaccounted for."

"You searched the tunnel?"

"Yes, Major. And the train. They must be in the cargo hold."

Major Savitch broke into a grin. "Then I shouldn't keep them waiting. Time to say hello to our guests."

He reached up for the handrails and pulled himself into the train.

In the freight wagon, Moss was pacing past the large wooden crates. He slowed and rapped his knuckles on the top of the nearest box. It gave a hollow sound; whatever was inside was not filling all of the space.

The Austrian commandos had their eyes fixed on him.

"What?" Moss said. "I'm not allowed to touch a box? Why doesn't someone tell me what's inside, so at least I'll know why we're in this mess?"

"Andy, leave it," Sunny said, from her position by the door.

"No, really. I think we have a right to know."

"You should listen to your friend," Friedrich warned. "Technically, you shouldn't even be here."

"What does that mean?" Sunny asked, her instincts kicking in.

"It means—"

"No," Mertens cut in. "Say nothing."

"What difference does it make?" Friedrich said. She turned back to Sunny. "You two were only added to the schedule last night. No one knew anything about it until you showed up and the paperwork landed at the same time. You are not officially part of this mission."

"Too right," Sunny said. "We're observers only. At least, that's what we were told."

"Only someone wasn't telling us everything," Moss added. "And now we're caught up in this, without anyone telling us what 'this' is."

"And I suggest we keep it that way," said Mertens. "The less you know the better."

11:25

"Oh, no," Sam said, tapping keys on the console moulded around his seat in the back of the motor home.

"What is it?" Arun asked.

"Park police. They're on their way. We weren't allowed to drive down here in the first place, remember, and we're definitely not allowed to drive on the grass. I did try and warn you."

"Oi, MANDROID," Donna called. "How long before the feds reach us?"

From monitoring their call traffic and calculating the signal strength differential, about thirty-two seconds.

"And time to take off?"

Twenty—

"Do it now!"

The camper van had parked behind a large, sprawling oak, shielding it from view, which was fortunate because what happened next would have had an observer rubbing their eyes in disbelief. A ripple pulsed across the surface of the vehicle and it seemed almost to melt in its wake, flattening out, spreading laterally while elongating at the front end, pushing the cockpit forwards. In seconds, the camper van was gone, reconfigured as a sleek blue and gold aeroplane. Rocket thrusters beneath the wings swivelled to point their exhausts downwards and, with a roar, the engines fired, pushing the aircraft away from the ground. The MANDROID plane lifted into the sky, hovered for a second, then turned and blasted away.

At the same time, a Royal Parks police patrol car pulled up and two officers got out, looking around in bewilderment. They could see tyre tracks leading across the grass from the road – and a number of scorch marks – but no vehicle.

Major Savitch strode through the dark train carriages, his heavy combat boots sounding out every step. He arrived at the freight wagon door where his men had positioned extra lighting. They snapped to attention in his presence.

Savitch reached for a fire extinguisher and struck the base against the steel door three times. *KLANG-KLANG-KLANG!*

"Little pigs, little pigs, let me come in!" he roared. "Or I'll huff and I'll puff and I'll blow your house down. Knock once to confirm you can hear me."

A dull thud came from the other side of the door.

"Excellent! Here is how it is going to work. You can open the door now and save us a lot of time and trouble. Or you can stay in there until I force you out. Just so you know, your colleagues are being kept at the front of the train and are all unharmed, for now. As an added incentive to help you make the right choice, I will be executing one of your commandos every ten minutes."

He addressed his waiting troops. "Keep watch on the door. No one goes in or out. Radio me if anything changes."

"Yes, Major!"

Inside the freight wagon, Mertens was on his feet, taking a quick inventory of his weapons.

"What's happening?" Sunny asked.

"You heard those animals. I'm not going to sit in here while they kill my men, one by one."

"Do we have a choice, because it doesn't look like it?"

Mertens exchanged a look with Friedrich. She nodded.

"There is a way out," Mertens said.

"What? Since when? I thought you said we were all trapped in here," Sunny said.

"That's what I want our captors to think, too, but there is an escape hatch, for emergencies. I'm going to try and

67

rescue my team but I can't do it alone. Who's coming with me?"

Corporals Schäplitz and Buhringer both stood up.

"We have direct orders to protect the cargo," Friedrich said. "That is the primary mission objective. Everything else is secondary."

"Even it means the lives of all of our team?"

"Yes, that's exactly what it means. We're all expendable."

"I'm going. You can stay here with the English if you want. Or they can protect the cargo."

Moss raised his hand to speak. "I'm willing to stay here with my colleague and we'll guard this wagon if it helps."

"Agreed," Mertens said. "And thank you."

"We should stick to our mission," Friedrich said. She glared at her team members, who avoided her angry look.

Working together, the commandos heaved one of the palleted crates aside to expose a square of wooden floor. Mertens knelt and pressed a knot in the wood. With a click, a floor section popped up by half a centimetre. Gripping the raised edge, the commandos lifted the panel to reveal a circular hatch set into the steel floor below.

"That leads straight down, on to the rail tracks," Friedrich said. "I'm going, too."

"You changed your mind quickly," Mertens said. "I

thought you were staying here with our new friends."

"You'll need all the help you can get. I'm going. That's final."

"As you wish." Mertens turned and spun the handwheel to unlock the door. He raised the hatch and said, "Lock this after we leave and don't open it for anyone. Understand?"

"I understand," Sunny said. "Good luck, all of you."

Mertens lowered himself through the hatch, landed silently on the sleepers below and dropped flat on his stomach. He crawled along the tracks, towards the front of the stationary train, followed by the other three Jagdkommando officers.

11:34

"How far is it to Austria?" Donna asked.

"I thought you were the navigator," Arun said. "Shouldn't you know?"

Donna sucked her teeth. "I didn't choose this chair. It chose me."

"It's about seven hundred miles," Sam said, from the back.

"I knew that," Donna said.

"How long is it going to take us to get there?" Arun said.

"We can go hypersonic," Sam said, tapping on the console. "It's a massive fuel burn, but Mach five would get us there in eleven minutes."

Donna did the maths in her head and laughed. "Four thousand miles per hour? Yeah!"

"It might draw some attention," Sam said.

"Not if we stay high in the sky," Donna said. "No one's going to see us, especially going that fast."

"That's not what Sam meant," Arun said. "You can't hide a sonic boom."

"I thought Quinny said we had to get there as fast as possible."

"Sam, how noticeable would it be?" Arun asked.

Sam tapped out some quick calculations and scratched his head. "We're relatively small, with a streamlined profile … so if we get high enough first, then it won't be as bad. The good news is we're not going to break any windows. The bad news is that for anyone underneath, it's going to sound like a massive bomb going off over their heads."

Donna grinned. "Cool. What are we waiting for? We have our orders."

"We're going to burn some serious juice, though," Sam said.

Arun smiled lopsidedly, his eyes shining with excitement. "We'll take that chance. Fasten seat belts. We're going to get some serious G's, my g's. MANDROID, take us to Mach five."

"It worked," Sunny said to Moss as soon as the escape hatch in the floor was sealed again.

"What worked? I don't know what you're talking about," Moss said.

"Andy, how long have I known you? Since when are you

going to miss out on the action? 'I'll stay here and help guard the wagon,'" Sunny mocked. "Ha!"

Moss smirked. "You should've been a police officer. OK, you got me."

Sunny rapped her knuckles on the top of the nearest crate. "Now the guard dogs are out of the way, let's find out what's worth hijacking a train for."

Back in London, at Secret Intelligence headquarters, Quinn was gazing out of the window while holding a steaming mug of tea. Burgess tapped away at the workstation, headphones covering his ears.

"Any word on the brats?" Quinn asked. "Or are they still arguing about who gets the window seat?"

Burgess held up a hand for quiet while he listened and toggled through multiple screens. He took off the ear cuffs. "As expected, the Austrians have mounted a full-scale recovery operation. They've got all the emergency services on site and are calling in heavy machinery."

"Do they know which train is stuck in the tunnel?"

"They know it's not a passenger one but, from what we've picked up, no one seems aware of the significance yet."

"That'll be because no one's telling them. You can

72

be darned sure their top brass know what's going on, especially with their Jagdkommando boys on board."

"Sir." Burgess stood to look over the monitor, meerkat style. "What *is* on that train, anyway? Why would it need armed troops and the mini war that's about to take place?"

"Forget that. I want to know where those flaming kids are."

At that exact moment, a thundering crash tore the sky to shreds, rattling the windows and making Quinn spill tea on himself.

"What the flipping heck was that?" Quinn bawled.

"Sounded like a sonic boom to me, sir," Burgess said. "They must be on their way."

11:38

Recessed wall lighting illuminated the curved walls of the Kallstein railway tunnel. The stalled train sat, a dark husk, with little reflection from its dull steel surface.

Underneath the train, grateful for the deep shadows, the four Austrian commandos crawled, following the sleepers towards the front of the train. Mertens was up front, with Friedrich next, then Schäplitz and Buhringer.

Mertens froze and signalled a stop, as two pairs of boots clumped past, heading towards the back of the train. He waited until they had gone before resuming the long crawl to where his fellow commandos were being held.

K-RAKKK!

Moss jumped, bringing his full weight down on the makeshift crowbar he had levered into the join where the lid of the crate was nailed in place.

"It's working," Sunny said, while Moss stopped to catch his breath.

"I just thought of something," Moss said, wiping his arm across his glistening forehead. "What if it's booby-trapped? Or it's something dangerous?"

"You thinking A, B, C?" Sunny said.

Moss looked baffled. "The old Jackson 5 song? What's that got to do with it?"

"No, dummy." Sunny shook her head. "Didn't you do any of the reading Mr Quinn gave us?"

"I might've skipped that bit," Moss said, looking sheepish.

"A, B, C: the three big methods of mass destruction. Atomic, biological or chemical."

"Oh. I don't think so. There are no hazard symbols on the crate and it's bog-standard wood, nothing fancy about it. I'm sure if this was toxic, they'd put it in a sealed container."

"Let's hope you're right." Sunny came over and added her weight to the steel bar. "Let's try again. Three ... two ... one..."

KKRRUNCHH!

This time the lid lifted, accompanied by the screeching of nails. Moss heaved the cover up and slid it aside. He looked into the crate.

"Oh. My. Gosh," he said.

* * *

High in the stratosphere, cruising five times faster than the speed of sound at 26,000 metres altitude, the MANDROID hypersonic jet tore through the skies above Central Europe.

Pressed deep into his seat by the acceleration, Arun scanned the various readouts on the head-up display in front of him. Beyond the graphics, the view in front ranged from the dark blue-black of near space, down to the azure blanket of the ozone layer and the white curvature of cloud below.

"How are we doing, navigator?" Arun said.

"I told you, that's not my job," was Donna's retort.

"You have the displays," Sam said, from behind her. "You can call up the holographic 3D maps. There's all kinds of overlays—"

"All right, all right," Donna said. "If it'll shut you up." She tapped instructions into the keypad on the arm rest. "We're over Germany."

"Cool! I've always wanted to see Germany," Sam said.

"Well, you're not going to see much of it from up here," Donna said. "Where we going again?"

"Austria," Arun said. "To the Alps, which run along the western border."

"Now might be a good time to ask, does anyone speak

76

German? That might be useful," Donna said.

I do, said MANDROID. *I have been programmed with all known human languages and can provide instantaneous translation services, should they be required.*

"You're kidding me! You can speak any language?"

That is correct.

"Do you know swear words?"

Of course.

Donna laughed. "This thing gets better and better."

11:41

Major Savitch marched down the aisle to the guard positioned outside the first passenger car. The soldier snapped to attention.

"Anything?" Savitch asked.

"No, Major. The prisoners are all still down from the gas and sleeping like babies."

"So that leaves just the four in the cargo truck, although I doubt they'll be there much longer."

"Sir, how can you be so sure they'll come?"

"Trust me. I know what it's like to work in a Special Ops unit. Your team becomes your family. You cover each other's backs. You watch over each other's children. That's why it hurts so much to lose anyone. Would you abandon a family member in danger?"

"No, sir, I wouldn't."

"Exactly. They will come and we will be ready."

Directly below Savitch's feet, Mertens stopped to rest. His elbows and knees were raw from crawling over the sleepers and ballast. He had been counting carriages and knew the wagon in front was where his teammates were being held, according to Savitch's words when he was taunting them.

Friedrich crawled alongside him and whispered, "Are you sure about this? If we can secure the passenger car, then what?"

"We defend our position and hold them off until help arrives."

"Didi, we're heavily outnumbered and we're taking these guys on their own turf. It's a terrible plan."

"I'm not letting my people be executed by these animals. If you don't like it, go back. Or do you have a better idea?"

"Is that real?" Sunny said, leaning closer to peer into the opened crate.

"It has to be," Moss said. "Otherwise, what's the point of all this security? Here, let me see how heavy it is."

He reached down, closed his hand on the cool metal surface and lifted the 12-kilogram gold bar.

"Oh, that's real all right," he said, grinning. "Pure, solid twenty-four-carat gold. Wow."

"How much do you think it's worth?" Sunny said.

"It would depend on the market, but probably around

eight hundred grand."

"For just one bar?"

"Yeah. I wonder how many there are?"

"Let me see…" Sunny quickly did the calculations in her head. "There's ten bars packaged in here and it goes five deep … so that's fifty bars in this crate."

"And there are eight crates, so four hundred gold bars."

"At eight hundred thousand each? That's well over a quarter of a billion pounds."

"That explains a lot," Moss said, "about why someone would want to hijack this train and why Quinn would want us on board, although I'm not sure he'd be doing cartwheels if he could see us right now. There's not a lot we can do while we're trapped in here."

Sunny leaned back against the wall of the carriage. "Andy, there's something else you should know, but you're not going to like it."

Norbert Janssen, chief of the Kallstein Fire Department, ran his fingers through his silver hair. In thirty years as a firefighter, he had only ever dealt with a single rockslide and that was after heavy rains had washed out a road. Now he had to deal with two and these were on the side of a mountain, with a freight train trapped in the middle.

Emergency vehicles were clustered along the rail track but there wasn't anything police or ambulance crews could do.

The distant cries of excited holidaymakers from the resort on the far side of the mountain carried on the chill breeze. Winter sports had quickly resumed since the rockfall was below the ski slopes.

Janssen squatted to get another angle on the stack of rocks blocking the eastern mouth of the tunnel. The largest boulders were the size of a compact car, the smaller ones in football territory. It had taken him the better part of an hour to drive up the winding mountain road from town, and that was in his Mercedes G500 4x4. It would take another couple of hours before heavy machinery could be brought to site, and it would need a bulldozer and mobile crane at the minimum to begin clearance work. He straightened up, wincing as his knees creaked, and crunched back to the warmth of his car. Once there, he reached for his radio. "Thomas, what do you have for me?" he said.

"How's it looking up there? Is it a big one, or just a few stones? You know what these train drivers are like," said Thomas, back in the cosy office. "Any excuse to take a break."

"You know what the train tunnel looks like?" Janssen said. "Now picture enough rock to completely block that, and then add the same amount again on top. It's that bad."

Thomas let out a low whistle. "I've managed to get you two bulldozers, pulled from the A12 roadworks, and a forty-tonne, all-terrain mobile crane is on its way from Rosenheim. They'll arrive in about an hour."

"Another hour?" Janssen glanced up at the tattered shreds of grey cloud scudding past. "We may have some incoming snow, and it gets dark quickly up here. Better send some generators and lighting, too. It's going to be a long night."

"I don't think we really want to be going to some of these places," Donna said, reading off the graphic displays around her seat. "You seen the names?"

"What do you mean?" Arun asked.

"We have Bad Häring, Bad Hofgastein, Bad Mittendorf... See? All bad. No good places. MANDROID, what's that about?"

Bad is the German word for 'bath', MANDROID replied. *In this context, it denotes a spa town, with mineral waters for health tourism.*

"Did you say spa town, as in resort? Like with heated

pools, saunas, massages, facials?"

That is correct.

Donna brightened. "All right! Maybe we can pay a visit while we're here."

"No way," Sam said. "How long till we arrive?"

"Couple of minutes," Arun said. "I can see a mountain range ahead. That must be the Alps."

"OK," Sam said. "MANDROID, we need to slow it down. Bring us in really easy so we can do a recce of the area."

Aye-aye, Captain.

Flaps opened on the sleek delta wings, creating instant drag to slow the aircraft before it began its descent.

11:44

"We're running out of time," Mertens whispered, huddled beneath the train carriage. "He said he'd start executing people at any time."

Friedrich nodded. "We need to hit the carriage at both ends. We know there's at least one guard. How about two of us take the front and the other two take the back?"

"That might work, but there's still a lot of risk," Schäplitz said. "Too many things can go wrong."

"I know what will work, to reduce that risk," Mertens said. "A diversion. If one of us draws their attention, the other three can secure the carriage."

"That sounds more like suicide," Friedrich said. "We have no idea how many of them there are. We're better off staying together."

"What's our objective here? To rescue our team. What's the best way to achieve that? By facing a focused enemy or a distracted one? It's the only way."

"I agree," Buhringer said. "It's a crazy idea but it does make sense."

"It's settled, then," Mertens said. "I'll create a diversion while you three hit the carriage. Take up defensive positions and hold it until help can arrive."

Friedrich shook her head. "I don't like this at all."

Back in the freight wagon, Sunny was gathering her thoughts.

"What is it you want to tell me?" Moss asked, leaning against a wooden crate.

"I haven't got this all worked out yet, so I'm not even sure how to say this, so just hear me out, OK?" Sunny said.

Moss nodded.

"You remember when I opened that flap to see the mountains whizzing past, before Friedrich told me off? And then we took that long curve before going into the tunnel?"

"Yes," Moss said slowly. "And then someone hit the emergency button."

"To alert the driver to the rockfall that had just happened," Sunny said. "But here's the thing. How could anyone on this train have known what was happening five kilometres ahead? We have no windows, it's a curving tunnel and even the driver can't see that far. That's what's been bugging me. How could anyone have known to stop

85

the train as soon as we entered the tunnel? Someone had to have hit the alarm or pre-warned the driver."

Moss scratched his chin. "What you're saying is someone on board must have known what was about to happen, that they're working with these trainjackers?"

"Exactly," Sunny said. "We have a traitor in our midst."

Back in London, at SIS headquarters, Quinn leaned over Burgess's shoulder to peer closely at the topographical map of Austria on his computer screen.

"They're approaching the incident zone," Burgess said. "Slowing down and dropping altitude."

"What's the situation on the ground?" Quinn said.

"Emergency services are there, as you'd expect. They've set up a cordon. Weather's turning bad, which is why you haven't got news or rescue choppers in the air yet. There's a TV crew prepping for—"

"Now that, I don't like." Quinn interjected. "What's the official story?"

"There isn't one. No one knows anything. All the press is being told is that a rockfall has closed the tunnel, nothing unusual. The authorities are keeping quiet about a train being trapped inside."

"Get on to BVT and have them do some damage control.

This is their mess."

"BVT?"

"Austrian domestic intelligence agency. They do what we do, only in Austria. Have them put a tame geologist on TV to say it's a natural event and get them to hold off from sending in their troops."

"Sir, it's their jurisdiction. How am I going to stop them sending in troops?"

"Tell them we have agents in the field and it's under control. And get *S.T.E.A.L.T.H.* online."

"How best do we do this?" Arun said, from his cockpit seat. "We're supposed to stay out of sight."

"That's not gonna happen," Donna said. "Can't dig out a train from up here. Unless you want to fire rockets at it. Hey, can we do that?"

Alarmed, Sam tried to redirect the conversation. "We should approach from the air, scan the area to get an idea of the situation, and then get close."

"Sounds like a plan to me," Arun said. "MANDROID, take us down."

Yes, Commander. But first, I have an incoming communication.

"Uh-oh."

"*S.T.E.A.L.T.H.* team, this is Old Spice. What is your status?" Quinn's growl filled the cabin.

"Well, we're here," Arun said. "We made it, in under fifteen minutes."

"Do you want us to get you a postcard?" Donna said. "Or we could bring you back a sausage? Isn't that, like, a thing over here?"

"I didn't send you on a sightseeing trip! I want you on the ground and getting my agents back safely. Got it?"

Donna scowled. "You know, you're going to have to work on your attitude, Spice Man. All this barking at people and giving orders isn't going to make them want to do you any favours, you know."

Old Spice has ended the call, MANDROID reported.

"Bit rude," Donna said.

"You really shouldn't wind him up," Sam said. "He's bailed us out of trouble before and we need him for cover."

Arun nodded. "He's on our side."

"Maybe," Donna said. "I still don't trust him."

"You don't trust anyone," Arun said.

"That's not true," Donna said to herself.

"It looks like we have a ski resort on the western side of the tunnel, above the site of the second rockfall," Sam said, scanning his screens as the MANDROID plane circled high above the disaster zone. "The train tracks are below, to the south. Let's follow them east to the other side."

Fire Chief Janssen took a sip of hot black coffee from his flask. He had the car engine running to heat the cab and he stared at the blocked tunnel entrance. The rockfall wasn't an accident. One might have been, but two was an impossibility, which meant somebody had deliberately sealed off the tunnel at both ends. Had they known a train was inside at the time and, if so, was that the intention? To pull off such a feat would require resources, skills, training and a purpose, which left the question of why?

Janssen was jolted out of his musing when the surface of his coffee started trembling like the skin of a jelly. The engine was making a strange noise, too. He closed the flask and killed the motor. The sound continued, so it wasn't coming from the car after all. He jumped out of the cab, spinning around to home in on the source of the thundering roar, growing louder. And then he looked up to see the silhouette of a sleek aircraft hovering ahead.

"*Was zum—*"

Without lights or markings, Janssen had no idea what it was or where it was from. All he knew was that it was making an unauthorised landing in his incident area. He reached back into his Mercedes and pulled out a megaphone.

"*Achtung bitte!*" he said into the speaker. "*Dies ist ein Sperrgebiet. Identifizieren Sie sich und geben Sie Ihre Aufgabe an.*"

Inside the MANDROID aircraft, Arun tried to make out the small figure below with the bullhorn.

"What's that bloke saying?" he asked.

He is warning us that we are in a restricted area and he is asking us to identify ourselves and to state our business, replied MANDROID.

"No kidding it's a restricted area," Donna said. "It's a disaster zone."

"I think he knows that," Sam said, looking at several screens on his console. He zoomed in on the red car with the white letters FEUERWEHR stencilled on the side. "He's from the fire brigade."

"We should tell him who we are and that we're here to help," Arun said.

"What, are you mad?" Donna said. "We're not supposed to be here. Think of something else."

"Can you think faster?" Sam said. "We have a new problem."

"What is it now?" Arun snapped.

"You see that van coming up the slope? It's a TV news crew. We can't let them film MANDROID. We should go. Abort the mission."

"No!" Arun said. "We only just got here. We've got a job to do."

Donna immediately took charge. "MANDROID, give me audio. And get the guns ready."

"Whoa! Donna, no! Whatever you're thinking—"

"Shut it, Arun. I'm an Admiral, remember? I outrank you."

11:53

Inside the tunnel, and underneath the first passenger carriage, the four Austrian Jagdkommando soldiers had taken up their positions. Schäplitz and Buhringer had crawled between the tracks to the front of the wagon, Mertens was positioned in the middle, and Friedrich crouched at the rear of the car in which their unconscious comrades were being held. With the clock running down, every second mattered.

Mertens held up his open hand, fingers outstretched. He tucked in his thumb, then his little finger followed by his ring finger, counting down. *Two ... one ... go!* He released the armed stun grenade in his other hand, sending it skittering across the concrete floor.

BLAMM!

A blinding flash of magnesium was accompanied by a thunderclap in the confined space. As Savitch's men reeled in surprise and shouts of confusion rang out, Mertens burst from cover, running past the front of the train while sending a spray of sub-machine gun fire high into the air. Several of the intruders gave chase, shouting into their walkie-talkies.

Friedrich steeled herself, saw a pair of boots hit the ground as the guard jumped down from the carriage, and made her move at the same time as Buhringer and Schäplitz.

She slid out, sprang to her feet and leapt up the step into the vestibule area, stubby Steyr sub-machine gun at the ready. Taking a breath, she yanked open the door – and stopped dead in her tracks.

Three carriages further down, in the sealed wagon, Moss rubbed his face with his hands.

"A traitor?" he repeated. "Who?"

"If I knew that, I might have done something about it," Sunny said. "Someone pulled the alarm to stop the train, well before even the driver could have seen what was happening at the front end of the tunnel, and so they must have known what was going on. Think about it."

"I am thinking," Moss said. "If they knew what was going to happen, then they would have been prepared for the knockout gas, so it must be one of the four commandos who are still free. Or it could be all of them."

Sunny shook her head. "No, if they were all in it together,

then they could've taken us out and thrown us in with the others. Whoever it is, they didn't want to blow their cover."

Moss scowled. "It could be two, then. We don't know."

"Stick to what we do know, detective," Sunny said. "Whoever it is, is outside this carriage with the others, where he – or she – can pick them off."

"And they left us in here, because we're not a threat. That's nice."

"It's also true," Sunny said. "Our mission remains to guard this gold. It's the only thing we can do."

On board the MANDROID aircraft, hovering 50 metres above the security cordon, the argument continued.

"Donna, stop!" Arun said. "We can't go round shooting up the place."

Donna ignored him. "MANDROID, do I have audio?"

Yes, Admiral. The personnel on the ground will be able to hear you.

"OK." She cleared her throat. "You, on the ground! Get that news crew out of my face. We're going to land this plane and I don't want anyone within two hundred metres, get me?"

"MANDROID, can you repeat that message, this time in German, and with the Dalek voice?" Sam added.

On the ground, Janssen struggled to make sense of what he was hearing: a child's voice had spoken in English, before a harsh robotic rasp had repeated the message in perfect German. What was going on?

"What's he doing? Has anything changed?" Sam called from the back of the cabin.

"Not that I can see," Arun said, looking down from the cockpit window. "MANDROID, is that news team filming anything?"

They have a camera recording but the view will be limited from inside the vehicle. At their current range, they will have insufficient resolution to determine any details but that will change soon.

"That's what I thought," Donna said, "so we have to keep them away. We don't exist, remember?"

"MANDROID, give me the loudspeaker," Arun said. "We can ask them again to clear off."

"No time for that," Donna said. "Arm the guns."

BEEP-BEEP!

Fifty metres below, Fire Chief Janssen turned at the sound of a car horn and saw the approaching news vehicle, a large van with a roof-mounted satellite dish.

At the same time, the aircraft hovering overhead spun

to face the truck. *BRAAAP!* Fire spat from rotary cannon beneath the wings and the snow erupted in front of the news vehicle.

"*Was zum?*" cried the driver. "It's shooting at us!"

"I didn't sign up to be a war reporter!" the camera operator said. "Get us out of here!"

The news van skidded to a stop before rapidly reversing the way it had come.

Shell casings rained down around Janssen, thudding softly into the snow. He touched one with his boot and stared at the aeroplane, tracking it as it came down to make a gentle landing beside the train tracks, its exhaust kicking up a cloud of loose snow and gravel.

Janssen raised the megaphone to his lips. "You have my permission to land," he said in English.

"Told you," Donna said with a wide grin.

"That's *not* how we do things," Arun said. "We *don't* go round shooting at people doing their jobs."

"Oh yeah? You didn't say that last time, when we were rescuing your dad."

"That was different," Arun said. "That was self-defence."

"So was this. They were shooting with a camera. Besides, it worked, didn't it?"

"That's not the point!" Arun was fuming now.

Sam's eyes were fixed on his console screen, which showed Janssen waving his arms to draw their attention. Arun and Donna were too busy arguing to notice.

"MANDROID," he said, "my turn for the audio."

Aye, Captain.

"And change this to German: Attention, ground people. We come in peace."

Donna and Arun both stopped in mid-sentence as the words echoed back from outside.

"Are you for real?" Donna said. "What next? Take me to your leader?"

In London, at Secret Intelligence headquarters, Burgess took off his headphones and beckoned Quinn.

"Sir, comms have intercepted chatter from a news crew over in Kallstein," he said.

"The news?" Quinn repeated.

"Yes. They're saying a strange aircraft dropped from the sky and when they approached … it opened fire on them."

Quinn dropped his face into his hands. "What are they trying to do? Start a war?" He composed himself. "Let's do damage control first to try and contain this. We'll need to quash that news story before they go on air, as

97

well as convince the Austrians that we're not conducting military operations on their turf. If we can pull that off, I'll be having serious words with those little brats."

11:59

Corporals Buhringer and Schäplitz slid open the door at the front end of the first passenger carriage and stepped in, sub-machine guns at the ready. They were expecting to see the rest of their Special Forces comrades propped up in the seats, perhaps restrained and with a guard or two. What they were not expecting was to see Petra Friedrich standing at the far end of the empty wagon, aiming her weapon back at them.

"Where are they?" Friedrich asked.

"Not here, that's for sure," Schäplitz said.

"It's a trap!" Buhringer said. "And we walked right into it."

"Clever boy," said a voice in his ear, and he felt the cold steel of a gun barrel press into his cheek.

Seeing two shapes appearing behind her teammates, Friedrich whirled with a roundhouse kick, connecting sweetly with the ribs of the man who was sneaking up behind her. She hit him again, landing a swift one-two with the barrel and stock of her gun and finished with an uppercut, sending him falling back out of the open carriage door.

Her training kicked in and, thinking quickly, she weighed her options. The carriage was compromised as a defensive location, her teammates were captured, meaning her only escape route was back the way she had come.

With a short run-up, Friedrich leapt through the doorway and landed on the human crash mat she had just positioned for herself before rolling to her feet.

She looked up at the sound of someone clapping and saw a half-dozen mercenaries had their guns trained on her.

"Nice moves, *fräulein*," said a stocky man with a V-shaped hat and a ribbon bar affixed to his black camouflage jacket. "Although a three-point landing would have been more impressive, but it is hard on the joints."

Friedrich glared back. "I know you," she said. "You're Ratko Savitch." She spat on the ground. "The Executioner of the East. You're a butcher, wanted in The Hague for hundreds of war crimes."

Major Savitch waved a hand, as if shooing away a fly. "Oh, that. Such old news. I've moved on to more … rewarding things. Now, put the gun down and nobody has to die." He snapped his fingers and two of his men marched Schäplitz and Buhringer to the front, each with a pistol to the throat.

"Where's Mertens?" Friedrich demanded.

"The other one? We'll find him soon enough. It's not like there are that many hiding places in a sealed tunnel. I'll say it a second time: put the gun down. I won't ask again."

"Friedrich, don't do it," Schäplitz said. He heard the soft click of the pistol hammer ratcheting back beside his ear.

Her nostrils flaring and mouth twisting, Friedrich flung her Steyr sub-machine gun at Savitch's feet.

"You came to find your captured colleagues," Savitch said. "Consider your mission accomplished." He gestured to his men. "Put them with the others. You know the plan."

"Yes, Major."

The whine of engines died down as the MANDROID jet settled in a pond of melted snow.

Janssen leaned against his car and raised the megaphone to his lips again. Before he could speak, a metallic rasp reverberated around him.

"Sir, please use the radio in your car. There's no point in having the whole world listening in," it said.

The Fire Chief blinked a few times, then tossed the bullhorn on to the back seat and climbed into his 4x4.

"Who are you and what do you want?" he said in English, into the car radio.

"Well, we're not aliens, and this isn't a UFO," the voice replied.

"I didn't for one minute think that was the case," he said.

"Oh, good. I think we may have got off on the wrong foot. We're here to help."

"By shooting at civilians? How can you help?"

"Maybe it's best if we give you a demonstration."

Inside the MANDROID jet, Arun spun his seat round to face Donna and Sam.

"What do you think?" he asked.

"I've done the structural analysis and geological evaluation," Sam said.

"Targeting's given us a weak spot by the tunnel entrance," Donna said.

"OK, let's give it a go."

"Hello?" Janssen said into the radio. "Are you still there? I thought something would have happened by now."

"You might want to move back," the metallic voice said. "And cover your ears."

"What? Why would I...?"

Janssen's words died away as he saw a hatch open below the body of the blue and gold aircraft and a small missile slide out. It launched and streaked across the clearing, whooshing above the rail tracks until it slammed into one of the largest boulders blocking the tunnel.

The ensuing explosion shattered the rock, blasting it into small lumps of rubble. One of them bounced off the bonnet of Janssen's Mercedes, leaving a dent.

"Yesss!" Sam cried, zooming his screen in on the boulder fragments.

"Did it work?" Arun asked from the MANDROID cockpit.

"It worked. Time for part two," Donna said. "MANDROID, switch to excavator mode."

The Fire Chief was reaching for his radio once more when a shimmer rippled across the sleek jet parked in front, and its shape seemed to melt and flow. The nose, wings and tail all shrank and moulded back into the fuselage, which thickened into a boxy shape. Wheels formed within emerging caterpillar tracks and a large, bladed shovel extended at the front.

Janssen shook his head to clear it and rubbed his eyes while the huge bulldozer trundled forward, lowering the scoop as it went and gathering up chunks of rock. Once the shovel was full, the blade lifted up, glided across the top of the vehicle until it reached the opposite end and dumped the tonnes of rubble on the ground behind it.

"So, what do you think?" said the voice over Janssen's radio. "Should we carry on, or do you still want us to leave?"

Janssen continued to stare at the futuristic vehicle in front of him.

"Can you still hear us?" the rasping voice came again.

"You're a bulldozer that can fly?" Janssen said at last.

"Among other things. We reckon we can clear that tunnel mouth in around an hour."

"I doubt that's possible, but be my guest and, by all means, prove me wrong."

"Cool. We love a challenge."

12:06

Lying flat beneath the train, Corporal Mertens froze as a number of boots marched past, heading towards the back of the train. He counted 10 pairs of legs, three wearing grey Jagdkommando camouflage and the others in black camo. That meant the rescue attempt had failed and he was now on his own. He had tallied 20 enemy troops so far, including the ones he had escaped from, although there could be more. In any case, he was outnumbered and the best he could do was to remain free until help could arrive.

He began crawling back along the tracks towards the armoured freight wagon.

At the rear passenger carriage, the door opened and the captured Special Forces soldiers were marched inside.

Friedrich, at the front, saw her other teammates propped up in the passenger seats, with zip ties around their ankles and wrists, and baggy hoods over their heads.

"Chloroform takes five minutes to knock you out and

a blow to the head might cause brain damage, so let's be nice and leave you conscious, OK?" the lead soldier said into Friedrich's ear.

He zip-tied her wrists behind her back, dumped a clean hood over her head and pulled the drawstring, before guiding her to a seat. He shoved her down, zip-tied her ankles and did the same to Schäplitz and Buhringer.

"This carriage is wired with explosives," he said to the prisoners. "Remain here and you will live to see your families, you have my word. If you disobey and get in our way, you will all die. That's how it is."

He slammed the door shut once more.

"Sam, how are we going to do this?" Arun asked from the front of the MANDROID cabin.

"I've run X-ray tomography and LIDAR scans so we have a three-dimensional model to work from," Sam said. "The granite boulders at the base are the hard part, but the top layer of shale and gneiss will be easier to shift since it's in smaller chunks."

"Seriously? We're just gonna scoop it up and dump it to clear the tracks?" Donna asked.

"Yes, but we have to be careful in case there's any more loose rock above that's waiting to fall."

"I've got a better idea," Donna said. "MANDROID, don't you have some kind of digging apparatus or drilling mode?"

Yes, Admiral. I have a tunnelling configuration.

"So why don't we just drill down under that rock and come up in the tunnel?" Donna said.

"Because we don't know what kind of structural damage the tunnel has sustained," Sam said, as if this was the most obvious thing in the world. "We could bring the whole lot down on our heads."

"Besides," Arun added, "there's probably a lot more people on that train. How would we get them out?"

"OK," Donna said, undeterred. "How about we drill through that rockfall?"

Captain, I have an incoming communication, said MANDROID.

Sam groaned. "Can't he just wind his neck in and let us get on with the job?"

"I heard that, Baby Spice," Quinn's voice barked in the cabin. "Give me the good news before I give you the bad."

Arun, Sam and Donna all looked at each other warily.

"Donna, you're the highest rank, you tell him," Arun said.

"Uh-uh. You're sitting in the front seat. I delegate to you, my minion," Donna said.

"Well?" Quinn said.

Arun scowled at Donna. "We're on site, we've done an assessment and we're about to start clearing the eastern tunnel mouth," he said.

"Who have you been liaising with?"

"There's a local Fire Chief, who seems helpful."

"And what about the news crew? Did it not occur to any of you geniuses that if you shoot at a television camera, they could film it and report it to the whole world?"

"Oh, gosh," Donna blurted.

"Indeed. Luckily, you've got me covering your back and I've managed to spike the story for now, but only on condition I give them an exclusive on the full story later. It's going to take some doing to leave you lot out of it."

"The Fire Chief's given us a two-hundred-metre cordon," Sam said.

"Make it five hundred. Tell them you're radioactive or something. And start monitoring transmissions. Block anything which mentions you."

"We can do that?" Arun said.

"Of course you can blimmin' well do that. Not much point in being a secret if everyone can blab about you. What's your ETA for extraction?"

"We're going to need about an hour to dig our way in. Then we can guide the train out, pick up your agents and get them home."

"Old Spice, how we gonna know which people are yours?" Donna asked.

"You'll know. And one more thing, and I mean this: no more missiles. There's a lot of snowpack up there and the last thing we need is an avalanche."

"Oops. We didn't think of that," Sam said.

"I noticed. Now, get to work. I'll check in later."

Fire Chief Janssen leaned forward for a better view through his windscreen. While he watched, the blue and gold bulldozer trundled up to the blocked tunnel mouth again, with the blade lowered. He couldn't be sure but it looked like the blade folded up into a long, conical shape with a screw thread spiralling around. The giant drill bit began to spin faster and faster before the vehicle advanced and drove the tip into a fallen slab. Black dust clouds obscured the view and the shriek of metal against rock echoed off the mountain walls.

"You know that's not possible," he said to himself.

In the tunnel on the other side of the drilling work, Vlado – one of Savitch's mercenaries – was stationed on lookout duty. A low rumbling sound made him move closer to the rockfall. He closed his eyes and listened intently. A grinding sound was coming from beyond the blockade, steadily growing louder – and then the point of a spinning blade broke through the mass of stone, scattering chunks of granite.

Vlado reached for his walkie-talkie. "Major, we have a problem."

12:18

"You know what I always hated most about being a detective?" Moss said to Sunny, as they both sat leaning against a wooden crate in the freight wagon. "The waiting around. It's like when you're on a stakeout and you reckon the suspect is going to show, but you don't know that for sure, so you're sitting there, with cold coffee and needing a pee but you know the moment you go, that's when he'll show, so you hold it in and he doesn't appear? *That.*"

Sunny had her eyes closed. "You know what I hated most about stakeouts? Being stuck with a partner who didn't know when to shut up."

"Ouch. I'll take that as a hint."

TINK-TINK!

Eyes now open, Sunny scrambled towards the sound. "It's coming from the escape hatch," she said, lifting the wooden cover.

Moss drew one of the Glock pistols he had taken earlier. "It could be a trap."

"True, but there are two other doors that aren't hidden.

Why use this one?"

The metallic tapping sounded again. *TINK-TINK!*

"Give me the other gun," Sunny said. Moss handed it over and Sunny tapped twice on the handwheel with the barrel.

A rapid tapping followed in response. *TINK-TINK. TONK. TINK-TINK-TINK. TONK-TONK. TINK. TINK-TONK-TINK. TONK. TINK. TONK-TINK. TINK-TINK-TINK.*

"Is that—" Moss started.

"Yes," Sunny said. "Morse code. It's Mertens." She spun the wheel to unlock the hatch.

Moss levelled the Glock. "Since when do you know Morse code?" he said.

"Air Force Cadets," Sunny said. "Back in the day."

The circular metal door lifted and Mertens hauled himself up.

"What happened?" Moss asked, keeping the pistol aimed at him. "Where are the others?"

"The rescue failed," Mertens said. "Friedrich blew it. She messed up the timing, went early, gave away our position. There were too many of them. I managed to get away but the others were taken."

"Where are they now?" Sunny asked.

"They're all at the back of the train, not the front. It

was a set-up."

"So when that bloke said 'first passenger car' and 'shooting starts soon', that was all a bluff, for our benefit?" Sunny said.

"Yes," Mertens said bitterly. "And we fell for it. We were played like fools."

Inside the cabin of the MANDROID excavator, the team was busy with the clearance works.

"We've broken through the biggest slab," Arun said. "Do we go again and smash up the rest?"

"I'm not so sure about that," Sam said, tapping a display. "I'm watching our power levels and if we're not careful we could bring a chunk of mountain down on us."

"OK. Let's switch back to bulldozer mode for a bit and clear some of the rubble."

"I have a question," Donna said, rotating her seat to face Sam. "You've been spending a lot of time in here, right, playing Captain Pirate and things like that...?"

Sam nodded and reddened at the same time.

"So, is this like your new best friend, or are you going to say it was all 'research', learning what it could do?"

Arun spun his seat round, too, waiting for the answer.

"It's not like that," Sam said weakly. "I started coming

here after school, not because of anything but … because I felt sorry for him."

"Excuse me?" Donna said, eyebrows raised. "You do know—"

"Yeah, I know he's not human or anything but he's still a person. He has character."

Arun and Donna exchanged glances but let Sam continue.

"OK, he's an AI, right? An artificial intelligence. Yes, he's built on algorithms and programmed responses, but he's also equipped for machine learning."

"Which means what?" Donna said.

"It means the more he interacts with us and the more information we can give him, the more he's able to piece things together himself."

"It's not exactly like that," Arun started to say.

"No," Donna said firmly, raising her finger. "Now is not the time to get picky about it. Sam, are you saying you were playing with it … to teach it stuff?"

"Yes," Sam said, his eyes lighting up. "I've been trying to help him sound more human. I've even been teaching him jokes."

"You're kidding me," Donna and Arun said at exactly the same time.

"No, it's true. Listen to this. Hey, MANDROID, why will you never go hungry at the beach?"

Because of all the sand which is there, replied MANDROID.

Arun shook his head while Sam cracked up. "It's all about the timing."

I see the joke is predicated on a pun around the idea of a picnic food but the premise is fundamentally incorrect.

"What is it on about?" Donna said.

You cannot eat sand so the joke is totally wack.

It was Donna's turn to laugh out loud. "Who taught you to say 'wack'? Never mind, just don't say it again. Scrub that from your memory. Delete."

Yes, big man.

"You're right," Arun said, a wary look on his face. "He is sounding more human."

"What makes it a 'he'?" Donna said. "You call a ship a 'she' and MANDROID's a vehicle. Hey, MANDROID, can you do a female voice?"

Of course. The frequency and pitch of my vocoder output encompasses the full range of the human voice, MANDROID said, sounding like an adult woman.

Donna laughed and clapped her hands. "Do husky."

How does this work for you? the AI said, in a deeper

female voice.

"No!" Sam cried. "That is so wrong. It's MANDROID, not WOMANDROID!"

Donna shrugged. "We could still call her 'Mandy' for short, even if you don't like it."

"Or 'Emma'," Arun offered. "As in 'Emma *ROID*'"

The scandalised look on Sam's face set Donna howling with laughter again, and Arun couldn't help but join in.

"Don't listen to them," Sam said to the AI.

Haters gonna hate, MANDROID said in agreement.

Another hunk of rock fell away, widening the shaft of daylight falling into the tunnel. Vlado took a step back, to remain in darkness. He put his mouth to the walkie-talkie.

"Major, I don't know how they're doing it but they're definitely clearing the tunnel," he said.

"That's not possible," Savitch said over the receiver. "They couldn't have got any heavy equipment up here so soon."

"I'm just telling you what I'm seeing."

"OK. This is not an … unexpected development. Time for the contingency plan. Alpha team knows what to do."

12:32

Back at the train, Savitch's towering second-in-command, Drago, stopped outside the front end of the freight carriage. He looked down the length of the train to the front. "We'll uncouple from here," he said, and two of his men stepped forward. One disconnected the air-brake hoses while the other ducked under the buffers, turned a screw to loosen the shackle holding the carriages together and unfastened the towing hook.

Drago gave a nod of approval. "And now we have two trains," he said.

Moss kept his ear to the cold metal wall of the freight wagon.

"It's stopped," he said to Sunny and Mertens, who were watching him quizzically. "Something was happening outside, something mechanical, like they were moving something heavy."

"I heard the clunk, but that was it," Sunny said. "What would they be doing out there?"

"Isn't that obvious?" Moss said. "They must have a way of getting this cargo out of the tunnel, otherwise what's the point? They've stopped the train, taken control of it, and are going to have to somehow get these boxes out. All we can do is to make it as difficult as possible for them."

Mertens tapped the partially opened crate. "Speaking of cargo, I see you've looked inside, so you know what we are transporting."

"Yes, sorry about that," Moss said. "I wanted to know what was worth all this trouble."

"Nearly four hundred million euros in gold bullion," Mertens said. "It's an interbank transfer. Ordinarily, they'd fly it over but with airport security the way it is these days, rail was seen as safer."

"They're probably right," Moss said. "Travelling at a hundred kilometres an hour with a small army on board, what could go wrong?"

"Who knew about the gold?" Sunny asked.

Moss grimaced at his partner's directness.

"Only Friedrich, as Team Leader," Mertens said. "No one else knew. I only know because she told me when we were going to rescue the others."

"No one else knew this was a bullion run?" Sunny said. "I guess that narrows down the suspects."

"I'm not understanding you."

"Sunny has a theory," Moss said, nodding at his colleague. "It's OK, you can tell him."

"It's an inside job," Sunny said. "You have a mole. It's the only way this could happen."

Mertens scowled. "Come on. You don't think Friedrich is involved with these mercenaries, do you? I've known her for six years."

"People get greedy," Moss said, "and a quarter of a billion pounds is very persuasive."

Mertens shook his head. "She did say there were money problems ... that her parents' farm was being taken back by the bank. But I never thought she'd do this."

"Well, someone helped them plan this operation and if she's the only one who knew about the gold..." Sunny said.

"MANDROID, how are you holding up, fella?" Sam asked from the back of the cab, which was swaying while the excavation work continued.

Power levels are at sixty-two per cent and all systems are operating normally, MANDROID replied.

Arun watched the mechanical arms operating through the front window. "You're doing a great job," he said. "I can see the top of the tunnel. Is there any way to speed it up?"

A quantity of explosive, correctly placed, would clear much of the obstacle.

"But we're not going to do that, are we?" Sam added loudly.

"No," Donna agreed in a flat voice. "We're going to keep on digging until that train is ready to roll on out."

High above the tunnel, on the western side of the mountain, looking down on the Kallstein ski resort, Savitch's Alpha team was busy: dressed in white camouflage gear, they scurried across the packed snow, digging holes into the frozen surface and dropping shaped explosive charges into the gaps.

12:41

BEEP-BEEP-BEEEEEEP!

Fire Chief Janssen dragged his eyes away from the tunnel clearance works and looked for the source of the noise. Flashing orange emergency lights blinked at him from the edge of the cordon he had set up further down the tracks.

He climbed into his 4x4 and sped towards the assembled vehicles, snow chains rattling on the tyres.

Through his windscreen, he could see a fire engine, ambulance, two police cars and the local news van. Just behind them, and trying to push their way through, were a mobile crane and a bulldozer.

"Right on time and far too late," Janssen muttered to himself.

He got out and scrunched his way to where one of his firefighters was beckoning him. Before he got there, Giselle Dallmann, a young reporter, cut in front.

"Norbert, what's going on here?" she asked. "Why is some unknown aircraft shooting at us? Is this a military operation? Is it true that a weapons test went wrong and blocked the tunnel?"

Janssen set his jaw and fixed his gaze past the reporter's ear.

"Did you hear me?" she insisted. "I have a right to know. I can't even get this story on air because of some random interference at this end and the network blocking me at the other. None of this is normal."

"You're right," Janssen said at last, his stance softening. "You do have a right to know. Get rid of the camera, kill any recording devices and do not share anything with anyone unless I tell you. Those are my terms."

"Agreed." Dallmann made a throat-cutting gesture to her camera operator, indicating for him to stop recording.

"Walk with me." Janssen skirted the cordon and lowered his voice. "We both know two landslides blocking a tunnel is no accident," he said.

"Is it true there's a train trapped inside?"

"No comment. I came up here for damage assessment and that's when an unknown aircraft dropped in. No markings, no identification."

"So you don't know whose it is?"

"Correct. It came to help. It … unloaded some heavy equipment and is clearing the tunnel."

"Come on, I thought you were helping me. There's no way a plane could land here without a runway, let alone bring in equipment. It was nowhere near large enough."

"I'm telling you what I know." Janssen glanced at his watch. "They estimate they can have the tunnel clear in about another half-hour. After that, we can reach the train, which may or may not be inside. We bring it out and then we can see about clearing the western side of the tunnel. Your story will be the successful rescue. Feel free to exaggerate my people's efforts." He waved his hand in the direction of the emergency services. "But no mention of the mystery plane."

"What? No! Are you joking? This could be the biggest story of my career. This could get me to Vienna, on national TV, instead of covering this backwater. No offence."

"You're not listening to me," Janssen said. "Those aren't my terms. They're from our secret helpers. If you haven't worked it out yet, they're jamming your transmissions and you've seen what happens if you get close enough to point a camera. Trust me, and stick with the rescue story. Otherwise you won't have a story at all and you'll be the crazy lady who saw a UFO once."

"Let me think about it," Dallmann said, pulling her coat tighter and stomping back to her camera operator. "I don't like this at all," she called over her shoulder.

"Nor do I," Janssen said to himself. "Nor do I."

"Sam, what's happening out there?" Arun called from his cockpit seat. A small section of the head-up display was screening footage of the staging area.

"It looks like they've brought in some moving equipment. I'm seeing a crane and a bulldozer," Sam said from the back.

"Should we let them help?" Arun said.

"Are you stupid?" Donna said. "And let them get up close and personal? We don't exist, remember?"

"Donna's right," Sam said. "We can do this ourselves." A small screen on his console showed an external view of MANDROID, back in shovel mode, piling a mass of debris into an embankment. "There's a few large slabs still to break up and then it's mostly sweeping up."

In the shadows of the half-cleared tunnel mouth, Vlado shielded his eyes from the sunlight streaming in.

"Major, it's me again," he said into his walkie-talkie. "You said to let you know when the tunnel was almost clear."

"Already? How?" came the reply.

"Beats me. There's something out there that's shifting

rock like it's *papier-mâché*. Some kind of machine but I don't have a clear view of it."

"Darn it." Savitch swore. "They're pushing our timetable forward, which isn't going to work. Time to slow them down."

On the mountainside, high above the ski resort on the western side of the tunnel, the Alpha team leader put down his radio and reached for the detonator. A line of explosives, strung like Christmas lights, stretched out beneath him, packed into the snow.

The excited cries and yelps of skiers on the slopes below hung in the air before he pressed the trigger switch.

KRRUMPHH!

Muffled blasts of C-4 explosive punched through the compressed snow, sending shock waves deep into the ground. Sudden cracks formed along the icy surface and the packed slab of snow started to slide. As it moved, it collapsed into smaller, faster-moving chunks, building up speed as it roared down the slopes towards the unsuspecting skiers below.

12:48

"Come on, you can do it!" Sam said in encouragement as two arm-like, diamond-tipped extensions from the front of the MANDROID cab pounded at a large slab of rock.

Inside the vehicle, shock absorbers and noise cancellation cushioned the impact but, having grown up around building sites, Sam could imagine the racket outside. Dust drifted upwards as the chisel points slammed into the stone, targeting weak points revealed by geoscopic scans.

KK-RAKKK! A fracture extended across the boulder before it split into smaller chunks.

Your attention, please, Commander, said the AI. *I have detected unusual seismic signatures on the western side of the mountain.*

"Seismic?" Arun said. "As in earthquakes?"

"Not up here?" Sam said.

I detect eight pulses occurring simultaneously, MANDROID said.

"Magnitude?" Arun said.

Each was around zero point five on the Richter scale.

"Eight mini-quakes at the same time?" Arun's eyes widened as the pieces fell into place. "Explosions?"

That is a correct supposition.

"You could've said that in the first place!" Donna said.

"Can you give me a visual?" Arun said. "Up on the screen."

A glowing, emerald-green grid overlaid on the windscreen, with wavy orange contour lines indicating the height of the mountain terrain. Eight red dots appeared in a tight cluster at the top, before a series of red concentric circles rippled outwards from them.

"MANDROID, this is the other side of the mountain pass, right?" Arun said.

That is correct.

"Which means that area below the explosions is the ski resort, where all those people are?"

That is also correct.

"Oh, crud."

An avalanche is like a flash flood, or a dam burst, only with snow cascading at speeds of up to a hundred kilometres per hour: thousands of tonnes of it hurtle down, slamming into obstacles and burying everything in its path.

The skiers, snowboarders, climbers and snowmobile

riders enjoying the slopes of the Kallstein resort stopped and looked uphill as one, searching for the source of the thunder they had heard rolling between the peaks. White plumes of ice crystals rising from the percussive blasts of the buried explosives were the only clue. And then the snowpack fractured, collapsed and flowed towards them like a deadly white river.

Happy cries turned to screams of panic and terror. Parents scooped up children and ran sideways, desperate to reach the comparative safety of the slower-moving edges. Others, already at the treeline, flung their arms around the nearest trunk and braced themselves for impact. A few adrenalin junkies aimed their skis downhill and tried to outrun the pursuing cloud of destruction.

The full force of the avalanche smashed into the chalet buildings, ski lodges and lift towers, splintering wood and rending metal. It rushed past in seconds, roaring like a demon across the lower slopes and flowed down over the rail tracks and the access road running alongside.

After the snowslide had settled, a haze of ice crystals hung in the air, obscuring the scene of devastation, and an eerie silence settled.

Watching through binoculars from his lofty position, the

Alpha team leader gave a satisfied smile as he watched the torrent of snow level off and spill over the railway far below.

"Perfect hit," he said to his three team members. "Now, let's get down there and finish things up. One more job to do and then we can retire as millionaires."

His men reached for their snowboards.

"Please tell me we didn't do that," Sam said, his face as pale as snow. "When that rock split..."

"Sam, we're good," Arun said, turning round to reassure his friend. "Loud noises don't cause avalanches and we're too far away. You heard MANDROID. Someone set explosives and did this on purpose."

"We dealing with terrorists?" Donna said.

"I don't think so," Arun said. "We've had two unnatural rockfalls already. This can't be unconnected."

"But why trigger an avalanche now?" Sam said. "What's the point?"

"Let's forget all that," Arun said. "Right now, we need to get over there. People will be trapped under the snow. If we don't dig them out quickly it'll start to freeze around them and they'll suffocate."

"Are we equipped for that kind of rescue operation?"

Sam said.

"We have to be. My dad designed MANDROID for search and rescue in all environments, isn't that right?"

Correct, the AI answered.

"Then what are we waiting for? Every second counts at a time like this."

"But we can't do that," Sam said. "We have very specific instructions for what we're doing. You heard Quinn."

"Stuff him!"

"I'm going to ask him. MANDROID, please get Old Spice on the line."

Fire Chief Janssen was organising his rescue teams ahead of entering the tunnel. They were running checks on their equipment and communications, ensuring it was all operational. The tunnel mouth itself was almost open when, for the first time since beginning clearance operations, the excavator device stopped.

Immediately, Janssen sensed something was wrong so he half expected the squawk from his radio. He reached for it.

"Yes, Thomas?" he said into the handset.

"Chief. There's been an avalanche, a big one, over at the resort. It's gone." Thomas spoke quickly, his voice bordering on panic.

"Slow down," Janssen said. "You're not making any sense. What's gone? The avalanche?"

"No, Chief, the resort. All of it."

12:51

At Secret Intelligence headquarters, on the South Bank of the Thames, Burgess adjusted the brand-new autofocus webcam he had just plugged into the spare laptop.

"That should do it, sir," he said to Quinn, who was leafing through situation reports.

Quinn grunted in acknowledgement and Burgess returned to his PC to check if anything had happened in the past few minutes. He jumped up in alarm.

"There's been an avalanche near the tunnel," he said.

A flicker of alarm flashed across Quinn's face. "Is the S.T.E.A.L.T.H. team safe?"

"I think so. They're calling you now."

Quinn hurried to the laptop to take the call.

Arun jumped when Quinn's craggy face appeared on the front windscreen in high definition.

"What is going on over there?" Quinn barked. "I send you on a simple extraction and you bury a town?"

"It wasn't us!" Donna shouted back. "It was probably

the same crazy people who dropped a mountain on your train."

Quinn let this sink in and softened his tone. "And what about that train? Have you cleared a way through yet?"

"Just about," Sam called from the back. "But isn't this more important?"

"More important than bringing back my agents? No, is the answer. You have one job, just one, so get on with it."

"You can't be serious," Arun said, his nostrils flaring with uncharacteristic anger. "There are people trapped in ice and snow who are going to die if we don't do something."

"They won't all die," Quinn said.

"How can you be so heartless about this?"

Quinn sighed in exasperation. "I don't expect a child to understand. There's a bigger picture you're not seeing. MANDROID is a top-secret British asset. It's bad enough you being over there in the first place. I can't have you carrying out rescue operations in broad daylight for a bunch of foreigners."

"Is that how it is?" Arun was raging now. "So what does that make me? Or Donna? Are we going to be 'foreigners', too, when it suits you? My dad built MANDROID for rescue and that's what we're going to do. I don't know why we're wasting time discussing it."

"Listen to me, you little runt. I'm in charge of this operation. You follow my orders."

"Not any more," Arun said.

"You can't fire us, big man," Donna added with glee. "You're not paying us."

"If you were, I'd quit," Sam said.

"And we're not in the army so you can't court-martial us, either," Arun said. "Over and out."

Quinn took out his rage on the webcam, yanking it from the laptop and bashing it on the desk. Burgess winced and decided it was a good time for a bathroom break.

"MANDROID, get us over to the resort side of the mountain as fast as you can," Arun said, his heart pounding from the exchange.

Yes, Commander, said the AI. *Switching to anthropomorphic mode.*

Outside, Fire Chief Janssen was working the radio, trying to summon as many emergency-service vehicles as he could to the Kallstein ski resort.

"That's what I'm telling you," Thomas, his dispatcher, said over the speaker. "I've got reports that the road is out of commission. The avalanche went over the rail tracks and spilled down across the service road."

"Then get the teams as close in as you can, and they'll have to walk it from there."

"Won't it be too late by then?"

The scrunching of rock from the tunnel entrance signalled the excavator vehicle reversing away. Janssen dropped the mike and climbed out of the car for a better view.

"Is that it?" he yelled, hands cupping his mouth. "You're done?"

"No, but we have a bigger problem to deal with," the harsh metallic voice replied. "We have to roll. You can get the train out. We'll do the rest."

The machine folded in its front arms and the shovel flattened and tucked inside. Flaps closed, sections shifted, panels slid aside and the central module reared upwards. Impossible as it seemed, two longitudinal segments extended sideways, separated and re-formed as limb-like appendages. Moving fluidly, the humanoid construct sprang to its feet, placed a hand on the top of the tunnel mouth and vaulted with athletic ease to land on the angled face of the mountain, before sprinting away.

"Chief, you still there?" Thomas asked. "I said it'll be too late by the time any help arrives, won't it?"

"Maybe not," Janssen said to himself. "Maybe not."

Charging along on two legs, arms pumping like an Olympic athlete, MANDROID sped across the mountainous slope. Inside, Sam was plotting calculations on a touchscreen map.

"The tunnel is five kilometres long and the resort is about five hundred metres further on," he said. "We'll be there in a couple of minutes."

"Why didn't we just fly?" Donna said.

"It'd take longer to switch in and out of flight mode and we're in a hurry," Arun said. "Every extra second could cost lives."

Deep in the tunnel, near the western portal, Savitch was directing his men. Everything was back on schedule and going to plan, with one exception.

His walkie-talkie buzzed. From the channel number, he knew it was Vlado, the lookout hiding in the shadows of the eastern tunnel mouth. "Yes?" he said.

"Major, whatever you did, it worked," Vlado said. "That special machine they brought in, it's gone. I think they withdrew it."

"How much rubble is left to clear?" Savitch said.

"Maybe thirty tonnes of rock and gravel. Most of the big stuff was removed or broken down."

"Good work. Keep watch and let me know if anything changes." Savitch turned his attention back to his men. "We're nearly done," he said. "Pick-up is in one hour and then we'll all be rich, so stay focused. Next task is to finish setting the explosives in the train. And hurry!"

12:55

MANDROID skidded to a three-point stop with one leg outstretched, the other knee and one hand down for balance as it rounded the final curve of the mountain pass. It reared up to its full 20-metre height and scanned the white sea of devastation in front.

A tidal wave of ice and snow had ripped through the resort, snapping trees, sweeping away timber-frame buildings and mangling ski-lift towers. Everywhere, the pristine snow was marked with dots of colour, from hats, scarves, skis, poles, gloves, snowboards and backpacks, either jettisoned by desperate holidaymakers trying to stay on top of the snow, or ripped free by the deadly cascade. Ice crackled as it settled and froze in the sub-zero temperatures.

Sporadic movement marked the first survivors, staggering in shock and beginning the search for loved ones. Cries for help and screams of distress cut through the eerie silence where there had been laughter and excitement minutes before.

Inside the MANDROID cabin, the team sat in stunned disbelief as multiple screens displayed the wreckage and misery.

"This is bad. This is so bad," Sam said, his eyes welling up.

Donna shook her head slowly. "There are children out there." Her voice was numb.

"Where do we even start?" Arun said, covering his face with his hands.

Shall I conduct triage? MANDROID said.

"Yes," Arun replied.

"What's triage?" Donna said.

"I don't know, but it sounds like the right thing to do."

On the eastern side of the mountain, Fire Chief Janssen sprang into action. He gunned the engine of his 4x4 and came to a sliding stop by the cordon.

Dallmann ran to meet him. "Is it true, Chief?" she said, eyes wide with alarm. "Was there an avalanche?"

Janssen pushed past her and went straight to the bulldozer, where the operator was keeping warm in the cab with the engine running.

"We can't do anything about Kallstein right now, but

we can get that train out and help whoever's on board," Janssen said to the driver. "Get moving!"

"I thought you didn't need me," the operator grumbled. "You had someone else doing my job."

"They're gone now, so you're up. Time to save the day."

Dallmann stood at his side while the 10-tonne bulldozer roared past, heading for the tunnel.

"Please," she said. "My sister took her family skiing today. Tell me they're safe."

Janssen removed his cap and brushed the snow off. "I … have some help on its way," he said. "We'll do our best."

Triage is an assessment to determine priorities for action, MANDROID explained. *I have identified three areas of immediate concern.*

"Go ahead," Arun said.

The windscreen head-up display changed to show a schematic of the battered ski slope. To the west lay the wrecked chalets and hotels; a line of cable cars hung on the east; and the railway line and service road ran to the south. Around a hundred glowing red dots appeared, scattered across the window.

Thermal imaging has identified heat traces of people trapped under the snow, said the AI. *I have pinpointed their locations here. However, core body temperatures are dropping fast.*

"What are we waiting for?" Arun said.

"Wait," Donna warned him. "There's two more things."

A photograph flashed on screen showing one of the many luxury ski lodges dotted across the resort, only this one looked like someone had taken a hammer to a matchstick house. A torrent of ice had slammed into it on one side, ramming it to the edge of a cliff where it teetered above a 500-metre drop.

The second priority is this occupied building, which has broken loose from its foundations, MANDROID said. *As you can see, it is in a precarious position and is in danger of falling.*

"I don't want to imagine what three could be," Sam said.

A new picture appeared, this time of the cable-car system, which ferried passengers up and down the slopes. The avalanche had missed most of the support towers, except one, near the base. The image zoomed in on a twisted steel pylon, with cables fixed to a headframe. The view panned across to show the bubble-like gondola of a cable car, swaying wildly, 40 metres above the ground.

Priority three is this conveyance. The supporting tower has sustained critical structural damage and will collapse in a short time.

"Oh, my gosh," Arun said.

"How did you decide which was most important?" Donna said.

I assigned a weighted value to each life in immediate danger and ordered them accordingly. Ninety-two people are buried in snow, forty-five took shelter in the building and fourteen are in the aerial conveyance. Others are less urgent.

"Let's get to it, then," Arun said, pointing at the map. "Here's how we're going to do this. We go to the cable-car tower, digging out as many people as we can on the way. Donna and I will get out and try to help the people trapped up there. That leaves MANDROID and Sam to get over to the chalet, digging out anyone else as you go. You two can deal with the building. Come on! Get moving."

The four members of Alpha team hiked over the rocks at the edge of the lower ski slope. The explosives experts had snowboarded down on untouched snow, keeping out of view behind a ridge, before reaching the stony ground above the rail tunnel. They were marching west towards the entrance.

"It's a shame we had to leave the snowboards behind,"

one of them said. "I wouldn't have minded surfing down that whole mountainside again."

"You'll be able to buy that mountain when this is over," his team leader said. "But first, we have one last demolition job to complete."

He led the way down to the fallen rocks partially blocking the western tunnel.

12:58

Back at the eastern tunnel portal, the heavy bulldozer dumped a scoopful of rocks and returned for another collection.

Fire Chief Janssen was on the radio again, coordinating with his office.

"The tunnel mouth is almost open," he said. "I don't have a clear picture of the west side, though. We had more space to work here, which is why it's where we started."

"You'll be pleased to know there's nowhere near as much rubble blocking the resort side. It'll be an easier clearance when you get to it," Thomas said, his voice emanating from the speaker. "I was getting reports from the resort. That was before the ... before I lost contact."

"I heard the access road was wiped out, so it's going to be a job getting over there to help. Can you get the army to send some choppers? Might be our only way in."

"I've put a request in but by the time they get there..." Thomas's voice trailed off. "And they'll be digging by hand."

"Just do what you can. I'm going to get that train out

and we can then use the tunnel, start clearance from the inside."

"Roger that. Let me try the army again." Thomas signed off.

Fifty metres away, cloaked in the shadows of the tunnel, Vlado pressed the talk button on his walkie-talkie.

"Major? The tunnel mouth is almost clear," he said, looking past the few remaining rocks at the bulldozer rumbling outside. "They're going to be sweeping the tracks in a few minutes."

"That's not ideal," Savitch said, "but we're ready. Find yourself a safe space. It's going to get noisy. I'm sending a surprise package their way."

SHHHHUUNKK! The fingers on each of MANDROID's hands had fused into a single block that then flattened and spread to form a metre-wide blade. With thermal imaging pinpointing the outline of a buried holidaymaker, the spade thrust powerfully into the snow, slicing deep. It levered 90 degrees and lifted, bringing up a mass of frozen crystals and the hunched form of a child. Dumping both on to the sparkling surface, it strode to the next target location and repeated the operation.

Eyes smarting from the sudden sunlight, the child gasped, shook snow out of her hair and clambered to her knees. "Mama!" she cried, searching frantically.

"Here!" The child's mother scrambled out of another pile of freshly deposited snow and staggered over to embrace her. Seconds earlier, both had been two metres under the surface.

SHHHHUUNKK! SHHHHUUNKK! SHHHHUUNKK!

MANDROID continued working its way across the snowfield, leaving tidy craters and stupefied survivors in its wake.

On board, Donna's screens showed other survivors pitching in to help. Some had avoided the ice flow, others had dug themselves out, and a few resort workers and guests had crept out from broken buildings. Donna zoomed in on her map displaying the remaining victims trapped under the snow.

"MANDROID, these people we're digging out, they gonna be OK?" she said.

Yes, Admiral. Vital signs are good for recovered survivors thus far. Some emotional distress is to be expected, along with superficial injury, but I detect no health emergencies, answered the AI.

"It probably helps that most people out on the slopes

are going to be in good shape to start with," Arun said. "You're doing great, big guy."

"Except for the bit about not being seen," Sam said, unhappily.

Meanwhile, in the freight wagon, Moss was killing time by doing push-ups.

"...Twenty-nine ... thirty..." He collapsed on the wooden floor. "I am so ... out of shape," he said, panting.

Sunny looked at him sourly. "You don't have to try and impress Dietmar. I'm sure he's sized you up already."

"What's that supposed to mean?" Moss said, propping up on one elbow. "Is he even listening?" He jerked his head towards Mertens, who was seated in a lotus position with the back of his hands resting on the floor, eyes closed and breathing in a serene manner. "Hey, Mertens. Hello! Earth calling! Do you read me, over?"

Without moving anything but his lips, Mertens said, "I can hear you, although I'd rather not."

"What else are we going to do?" Moss said. "We've been stuck in here for half an hour, just waiting. At some point, they're going to have to come for this gold. Until then...?"

"We wait."

Moss sat up and shot a concerned look at Sunny, as if

to say "is this guy for real?". "I know!" he said. "Let's play 'I Spy'. I spy with my little eye something beginning with 'g'."

"Gold," Mertens said, still only moving his lips.

"Wow, you're good," Moss said. "And you didn't even look."

"Andy, if we get out of this, remind me to kill you," Sunny said to Moss, her eyes blazing.

"You'll have to get in line," Mertens said.

"And they say Germans don't have a sense of humour," Moss said.

"I'm Austrian!" This time, a slight tightening of the eyes revealed a hint of irritation.

Outside, in the dark of the tunnel, Savitch was giving final instructions to Drago, his hulking second-in-command.

"Drago, you'll have only ten seconds to find a refuge, so get off as soon as you see one," Savitch said.

They were standing at the now-detached front half of the train, which comprised the engine and three passenger cars. The remaining mercenaries were all assembled by the rear half of the train.

"Understood, Major. I won't fail you." Drago climbed up into the driver's cab and started the engine.

Savitch nodded once and rejoined his troops.

13:03

"That's it!" shouted one of Janssen's firefighters. "It's all clear." He cut the flow to his fire hose and stepped back. He and other crew members from the parked fire engines had been blasting water at high pressure to sweep debris from the railway tracks.

Janssen flashed the lights on his 4x4 to acknowledge and reached for his radio.

"Thomas, it's clear. I'm going to go lead the group in on foot and locate the train. If we can bring it out safely, we will. I'll keep you posted. Over and out."

He stepped out of the car and strode over to his team.

"We're going in two by two," he said, addressing them. "You know the drill. Stay tight, stay close, stay safe."

"What's the latest on the ski resort?" Quinn said to Burgess, back at his desk in Secret Intelligence headquarters."

Burgess slid a headphone cuff off one ear. "Network traffic is picking up from survivors' phones. And the army are mobilising to helicopter in some rescue teams. They've got Mountain Rescue standing by to lead them in."

Quinn pursed his lips. "That's not good. It's one thing to have a bunch of oxygen-starved people claiming they were rescued by an alien — we can spin that as a hypothermia-induced mass delusion — but it's something else altogether to have the army in there. Imagine if they panic and shoot at the thing? Do you think Little Miss Hothead isn't going to shoot back?"

Quinn slumped and rested his hand over his eyes. "I really don't need this." His mobile rang and he checked the caller ID. It was C. Quinn groaned. "And I need this even less."

He put some distance between himself and Burgess and answered the call. "Yes, sir?"

"I've got a couple minutes between meetings, so I thought I'd check in and see how your *S.T.E.A.L.T.H.* team is doing."

"Thank you, that's good of you."

"And? How are they doing?"

Quinn hesitated, deciding how much he should say. "They're on site..."

"ETA for extraction?"

"We're ... working on that. Not long."

"You're equivocating. Just remember what I said, Quinn. If this goes off piste, you'll all be packing your bags."

"Yes, sir. Understood." Quinn hung up and looked back at Burgess. "Find out what those brats are doing."

SHHHHUUNKK! SHHHHUUNKK!

MANDROID deposited two more disoriented skiers on to the frozen surface. It had worked its way up the slope, moving east towards the twisted cable-car support pylon.

"How many is that now?" Donna asked from her middle seat.

"I make that fifty-three," Sam said, checking a screen. "Fifty-three who have seen us."

"We're nearly at the tower," Arun said. "How's that chalet holding up?"

The building's structural integrity is failing while the wind speed is increasing so the probability of it collapsing is imminent.

"Darn. Maybe we should have gone there first."

"No, Arun, you made the right call," Sam said. "That pylon isn't going to last long, either, and me and MANDROID will be able to get to that lodge pretty quickly."

Changing to default configuration to enable disembarkation, MANDROID said, coming to a stop near the cable-car support.

The humanoid shape seemed to stumble and fall,

compacting and reshaping in mid-drop; limbs folded in, wheels re-emerged and it resumed its familiar motor-home shape.

With the chairs now all at the same level, the seat belts unbuckled and slid away. Donna jumped up and headed for the hold.

Arun stretched and walked down to Sam, his legs stiff. "That's been a lot of sitting," he said.

"Arun," Sam said, his face deadly serious, "you and Donna aren't going to have me and MANDROID to help you. Be careful, OK?" He climbed out of his seat.

Arun wasn't sure how to react. He was touched by his friend's concern but the idea of a hug seemed too awkward, so he resorted to every boy's fallback option.

"I'll be fine," he said, and gave Sam a light punch on the arm. "Keep my seat warm, I'll be coming back for it."

Sam's face lit up. "Oh, yeah! I get to be in front now."

"Oi, Arun, we have a sitch," Donna called.

Arun found the short ladder leading down to the hold and slid down it to join Donna. She was holding up a ski jacket and a pair of salopettes.

"What's the problem?" Arun asked. "Wrong size?"

"No boots," Donna said. "There were some gloves chucked in the bottom, but this is basic stuff. School shoes aren't going to hack it in snow."

Arun winced. "It'll have to do. It'll be like going to school when it's snowed."

Donna narrowed her eyes. "I told you, I don't do cold."

"Then it's time to try something new," Arun said. "You also don't do friends and you don't help losers. See what happens when you start? One thing leads to another and next thing you know, you're happier."

Donna sucked her teeth in annoyance. "You don't know me, and who says I'm happy?"

"The fact that you've been smiling more without your face breaking in half is a clue. Come on, stop being so stubborn. I can't do this alone and there are people out there who need our help."

Arun snatched the jacket from Donna's hand and shoved his arm into the sleeve.

"Are you coming, or do I have to do this myself?" he asked.

"That's my coat," Donna said. "You get your own."

Two minutes later, the side door opened and Arun jumped out, followed by Donna. Their feet crunched on to the packed snow and a chill wind whipped around their heads. About 20 metres in front stood the creaking tower and, further along, the cable car, swaying dangerously.

MANDROID returned to humanoid form and reared up to walk away, then paused, flattened its hand into a shovel blade and speared the snow. It lifted and deposited the shovelful beside Arun, who could make out a half-buried red backpack.

"You might need that," Sam's voice blasted from the speakers.

With a wave, MANDROID strode away – *SHHHHUUNKK! SHHHHUUNKK!* – digging out trapped skiers as it went.

Arun brushed snow off the backpack and opened it. Inside, he could see climbing equipment, including rope, flares, a headlight, pocket knife, ice axe, heat packs and a bag of accessories.

"It's a shame there're no boots in here," he said, "but this is still going to be useful." He heaved the pack on to his shoulders and instantly regretted it as he sank into the frosty surface, gasping when snow filled his shoes.

At the bottom of the slope, at the partially blocked western portal of the rail tunnel, Alpha team was busily laying more explosive charges and detonator cord amid the rubble.

13:07

"Ugh, I hate the snow!" Donna complained, while she and Arun trudged towards the cable-car support tower.

"Yeah, I know," Arun said.

"And I'm freezing!"

"Yeah, I know."

"Let me ask you something," Donna said, plodding alongside Arun. "How many brown faces have you seen out here, skiing and stuff?"

"I don't think I've seen any," Arun said, unsure as to where the question was leading.

"Exactly! This is all white people's stuff. Even the snow is white. This is like ... ballet and opera. It's not meant for us."

"Like women's tennis and Formula One racing? And what about the Jamaican bobsleigh team?"

Donna laughed. "With proper, black Jamaicans? No way! There is no such thing."

"There is. Anyway, maybe you have a genetic predisposition to cold. You could even have German blood on your dad's side. Everyone's from somewhere else. Even the first Brits were brown."

"Well, if I do have some, it's not helping much, I'll tell you that."

They came to the base of the pylon, which was a lot taller and more daunting up close. Donna's eyes tracked the elevated cable along to the cable car, some thirty metres away. The biting wind buffeted it and the tower creaked with every swaying movement.

"That thing's barely holding together," Donna said. "How are we gonna do this, since it's your idea?"

Arun ran his hand through his mop of hair. "MANDROID said there are fourteen people up there. We have to get them down before this tower goes. That means we'll have to get a rope across for them to climb along, bring them to the tower and then down again."

"That part I figured out for myself. The bit you left out is who's doing the climbing?"

"I'll do that."

Donna looked Arun up and down, with fists on hips. "No offence, but you're a skinny wimp."

"Ouch. Say what you really think. You remember the time when I climbed out of that truck and along to the flat bed at the back?"

"Yeah."

"After that, I decided it would be a useful thing to do properly, so I got my dad to take me for some climbing lessons at the leisure centre."

"You know how to climb properly?"

"It was only three lessons, but yes, I think I can do this."

"You're not exactly filling me with confidence here, you know."

"It's our best chance. Unless you have a better idea."

Donna sighed. "Let's start climbing, then."

SHHHHUUNKK! SHHHHUUNKK! SHHHHUUNKK!

MANDROID deposited the last of the trapped skiers on to the chill snow and approached the rickety wooden chalet, seesawing on the chasm edge.

"We need to tread carefully," Sam said, sitting in the front seat and looking out of the cockpit window. "In case we disturb the snow."

I have already conducted deep radar scans and calculated depth and density of the snowpack.

"Oh, OK, then. Take us in for a closer look."

Aye, Captain.

As MANDROID drew closer, running multiple scans, Sam had a better view of the building: it had three storeys, with balconies on the upper levels, wide sloping eaves on the roof, like a flattened letter M, and was made mostly of wood, with some steel bracing. Snow was piled almost to the roof on one side, where the full force of the avalanche had hit, shearing it from its foundations and forcing it on to the cliff edge where it teetered.

"Remind me, how many people are inside?" Sam asked.

Forty-five. It would appear that some took shelter when they saw the avalanche starting.

"Why can't I see anyone? Shouldn't they be jumping out?"

Thermographic scans show some have sustained injuries but most are clustered in front of the wall furthest away from the cliff.

"Where the snow is piled up? That would block all the doors. Why would they all bunch up in there?"

I suspect the inhabitants have concluded that by concentrating their weight in that corner, they are serving as a counterbalance to prevent the building from tipping.

"They're huddling in one corner to weigh down that side of the building? Oh, crud. That means we can't just lift them out or the whole thing might topple, and then ... five hundred metres straight down on to rocks."

That is correct.

Five kilometres away, in the rail tunnel, Fire Chief Janssen led his crew of firefighters along the tracks. Daylight bleeding in from the tunnel mouth behind them gave way to dim overhead lighting.

The obvious expectation was that the train had stopped near the tunnel mouth, because that was where the driver would have seen the blockage ahead. But that was not the case.

"Why are we not seeing the train?" Janssen wondered aloud. "Why did it stop so far back?"

"Chief, do you hear that?" one of his team said.

Janssen stopped and listened: a low, rumbling sound was getting louder.

"Get off the tracks, now!" Janssen ordered. "Train!"

As the roar grew to a peak, the front of the train rounded the curve and bore down at speed. Janssen thought he saw someone jump from the driver's cab before he threw himself to the ground and rolled to safety.

The train hurtled past, approached the tunnel entrance – and exploded. Orange fireballs ripped through the engine and three passenger cars, shredding the train's metal skin and sending shock waves reverberating off the tunnel walls. The force of the blast tore a carriage off its axles and it rolled on to its side, dragging the other wagons off the rails. With a terrible screeching, grinding noise, the burning hulk crashed to a stop just inside the tunnel mouth.

Janssen raised his head to see a vision of hell: flames filling the tunnel and roils of black smoke billowing along the ceiling towards him.

13:15

An access ladder ran up the inside of the cable-car support tower. Ordinarily, a fenced compound at the base would have kept unauthorised personnel away but it lay in pieces, smashed by the avalanche, so Arun and Donna had taken the opportunity and started climbing.

"We should be using safety harnesses and double lanyards to clip on to the rungs a few steps above," Arun said, "but we don't have all that gear."

"So, don't fall, is what you're saying?" Donna confirmed from below him.

"Yeah." Arun's foot struggled to grip the icy metal rung and he silently cursed his school shoes.

The tower was 40 metres high and climbing it was hard going. It had started easily enough, but as Arun's limbs grew tired each step became more painful and his shins kept hitting the rungs. He stopped for a rest on a platform halfway up, to give his burning legs and aching arms a breather. Donna joined him and they drooped in silence, breathing hard and waiting for their thumping hearts to slow.

"Why are we doing this?" Donna said.

"Because we have to," Arun replied flatly. "People need help and we're the only ones who can do it. It's as simple as that."

"A lot of people would just walk away, you know. Say it's not their business."

"Donna, that's not who we are, and you know it. From the moment you offered to help me, you kind of gave yourself away."

"You really care about people, don't you?" Donna smiled.

"Something my dad said. If we don't try to be better, we might as well be animals."

"That must be why he built MANDROID, 'cause he's as soft as you are."

"Maybe. Ready for the rest of it?" Arun asked, returning to the ladder.

"Born ready," Donna said.

They continued the climb to the top, where the wind became a lot stronger, whipping at their coats. Arun stepped off the ladder on to another platform, shrugged out of the climber's backpack and opened it. He started sifting through the contents, laying out the various items on the metal grillage. Donna knelt to help, trying to ignore the gentle swaying of the tower and the creaking of the metal struts.

"I'm going to need this rope," Arun said, "those carabiners, probably the axe, and the knife. That should do it."

Donna watched Arun's face as he worked through the materials.

"What is it now?" he said, looking up and feeling awkward under her gaze.

"You really know what you're doing. This is, like, *another* Arun. Like the one I saw before, when you were so fixed on getting your dad back and nothing was gonna get in your way. I like that Arun. You're not like that in school."

Arun swallowed hard, then shrugged. "School's different."

He tied one end of the rope around his waist, threading it through the belt loops of his trousers, and handed the rest of the coil to Donna.

"That's not going to work if you fall," she said.

"It's not for that. When I get to that cable car, I'm going to tie it off at that end and I need you to tie your end here. Make it as tight as possible, no slack. Can you do that?"

"I know how to tie knots," Donna said. "Do you want a bowline or a figure eight follow through?"

"I'm not even going to ask how you know all that stuff."

Arun used a carabiner to clip the ice axe to his belt and climbed the hooped ladder leading up to the cross-arm, which extended from the tower head at a right angle like the jib of a crane. From this arm, a series of metal wheels were fixed in a line to support the thick steel wire from which the cable cars hung.

Inching his way to the edge of the cross-arm, Arun took a deep breath, knelt on the cold metal and reached both gloved hands out towards the suspended cable. Even though he had a good head for heights, it was still dizzying to be this high up, 40 metres above the ground. It was a long way down if he missed.

"Arun, be careful," Donna said, watching him from the platform below while playing out the rope.

While Arun stretched out his arms, the tower leaned again, almost throwing him off balance. He sprang back and wondered if the cable was supporting the tower rather than the other way round. The girders creaked from the strain before the structure righted itself once more.

He tried again, reaching out to grip the steel line with both hands and sprawled flat out, shimmying on his front, until he brought his torso to lie on the thick wire. He allowed his left leg to hang down for balance while bending his right knee and hooking his foot over so his laces rested on the cable. Then, he pulled with both arms while pushing off with his right foot and slid forwards, trailing the rope.

At the stricken ski lodge, MANDROID crept closer, its mechanical feet splayed to minimise vibrations and to improve grip on the snow.

Sam studied the various readouts flashing up on to the cockpit window.

"What do you think?" he said.

The structural integrity is compromised. Being constructed largely of wood allows some flexibility but this is offset by a lack of material strength.

"Meaning it's holding together because it can bend a little, but that's also stressing it?"

Aye, Captain.

Sam sighed. "Can we talk about the whole pirate thing for a sec?"

I have observed the continuation of our game is a source of tension between you and your shipmates.

"Yeah," Sam said. "I can tell they think it's a bit stupid. Childish, really."

And therein lies a flaw in their reasoning.

"Huh? No, they're both really smart."

Studies have shown repeatedly that those most able to advance the sum of knowledge possess a valuable trait: imagination. It is a characteristic which sets you apart.

"And that's a good thing, being a neek?"

That is why the Commander tasked you with the rescue of all forty-five people in the chalet. He trusts you to find a way.

Janssen burst from the mouth of the flaming tunnel, his face blackened and steam rising from his clothes. He dived on to the nearest patch of snow and rolled. At the same time, a firefighter marched past him, directing the barrage of water from a fire hose on to the burning wreck.

Like all trained personnel, Janssen had known to cover his head, hit the ground and move as soon as the train exploded. Now that he and his team had reached safety, he sat up and struggled to understand what had happened.

"Chief, you OK?" someone asked.

"No!" Janssen shouted. "I. Am. Not. OK." He hammered his fist on the ground with each word.

At the opposite end of the tunnel, hunkered down at a

safe distance, the Alpha team leader pressed the detonator button.

K-BOOMM!!!

The shaped charges his team had placed among the slabs and boulders blocking the western portal exploded, fracturing the larger rocks and blasting fragments into the sky.

The pieces clattered down through a dusty haze of pulverised stone. A gust of wind swept it aside to reveal a large opening in the stone barrier. Savitch's troops hurried to help finish the track clearance work from the inside.

13:21

Thirty metres doesn't seem like much until you have to drag yourself that far along a steel cable, Arun thought, trying to blot out the pain in his groin where the wire was pressing most. He had settled into a rhythm, pulling with his hands while pushing with his foot, creeping along like an inchworm. Pausing for a rest, he gauged his progress: two thirds covered.

"Arun!" Donna called from her position on the rickety pylon. "Your fan club is waiting." She pointed to the gondola cabin.

Arun followed her prompt and saw faces pressed up against the misted windows, staring excitedly at him.

KKRRUUNNKKK!

Just as Arun was pulling himself forward, the tower groaned and a judder swept through the lattice and oscillated along the wire. Caught half on and half off in mid-movement, his right foot slipped, throwing off his balance, and he pitched sideways, his body slipping off the cable. Instinctively, he tightened his grip and hung by his fingertips, 40 metres above the ground.

"We have to approach this thing logically," Sam said to MANDROID. "That's what the others would do. That chalet is like a big box with six sides, right, so the obvious thing to do would be to lift it. Do you have enough oomph for that?"

Theoretically yes, but the angled roof and its associated width would make gaining purchase difficult.

Sam rotated a 3D wireframe image of the ski lodge projected in front of him. "Yeah, I see your point," he said. "There's nowhere to get a grip."

And if there were suitable lifting points, the roof brace is too weak to bear the weight of the building.

"So all we'd do is tear the roof off?" Sam studied the building again. "What about the sides? Could we pull the thing?"

Given the gradient of the slope on which it is resting, that would not be an optimal solution.

"Why not?"

The building is partially embedded in snow. Once it is freed, gravity would prevail—

"Taking it over the edge." Sam rested his head in his hands.

"Your attention, please. I have detected a series of explosions at the western portal of the Kallstein railway tunnel."

Sam looked up. "What?"

"I have an incoming transmission."

"Why does everything have to happen at the same time?" Sam wailed.

Quinn's weary-looking face blinked up on the window display.

"Baby? What are you doing in the pilot's seat?" Quinn leaned closer, scanning the cabin. "And where are the other two?" His face reddened and a vein popped out on his forehead. "Don't tell me they've gone outside, not when your orders are to remain unseen."

Sam closed his eyes and hung his head.

"You're not answering me," Quinn snapped. "Hello?"

"Stop shouting at me if you want me to talk." Sam's voice was barely audible.

"Say that again?"

"I said, STOP SHOUTING AT ME!" Sam exploded.

Quinn froze, unsure what to do. "Oh-kay, then," he said warily. "No more shouting. Good?"

Sam nodded, looking like he was ready to melt down at any moment.

"Can I have a status report, please?" Quinn said, his voice calm and steady.

"It's horrible," Sam said, his lip quivering. "All these people were buried in the snow but we – MANDROID, really – dug them all out and they're OK now, even if they are foreigners to you."

"I didn't mean it like that. All I meant was that I'm putting my people—"

"Just stop. There's no 'my people' and 'your people' out here. Just people who need help and that's what we're doing, no thanks to you."

Quinn decided to let that go. "Posh and Ginger? They're outside, where they can be seen?"

Sam nodded again. "There are people trapped in a cable car that's going to fall. We couldn't be in two places at…" Sam's voice trailed away as movement outside the cockpit window caught his attention.

"Oh, crud! It's starting to go!" he said, watching a chunk of snowbank collapse beneath the chalet. No longer supported, the wooden building tipped towards the drop.

Sitting on the ground, while firefighters and other emergency crews bustled around, Fire Chief Janssen took a sip of coffee and glanced back at the flaming wreck of the train in the tunnel mouth. It had been a miracle that he and all of his team had got out safely, even if some were a bit bruised and battered, but he knew that if the intention had been to kill them, then none would have made it. There was something else happening here.

He creaked to his feet and stumbled towards his Mercedes 4x4, still parked nearby. As he walked, he reviewed the events of the past few hours. The day had started with a landslide at both ends of the tunnel, trapping a train. A mysterious vehicle had appeared and helped to clear the tunnel. Before it could finish, an avalanche had struck, wiping out the resort on the west side, which drew the contraption away. And then when he and his men went into the tunnel, the train hurtled towards them and exploded.

Firstly, Janssen was in no doubt that each supposed accident was deliberate. Explosives were the common factor in each: the rockfalls, avalanche and train; but why? Why trap a train only to destroy it? What was so special about this train to cause all this chaos? And then the penny dropped. Only *half* of the train had blown up: an engine and three carriages, all empty, so what had happened to the other half of the train?

Janssen started running, got to his car and grabbed the

mike for the radio.

"Thomas," he said to his dispatcher, "what's the story with those army choppers?"

"I have army reserves standing by and ready, just waiting on final authorisation. We'll have boots on the ground soon. I'm just praying we won't be too late."

"There's something else," Janssen said. "Tell them to come armed."

13:25

Savitch stood by the rear of the train, watching the circle of daylight at the western end of the tunnel. His explosives experts had blasted most of the blockage clear, and the rest of Savitch's troops had removed the remaining rubble by hand.

Drago, having jumped from the driver's cab of the train before it exploded and sprinted back the four kilometres, joined the Major. "Transport ... is on its way," he said between breaths. "Everything has gone ... exactly as planned."

Savitch allowed himself a tight smile. "Apart from the eastern tunnel clearance. That should have taken them much longer to complete and we wouldn't have needed to blow up the front of the train as a contingency."

"Maybe they got lucky ... and had a bulldozer nearby?"

"Maybe. Maybe not. I don't like not knowing. Let's get this cargo ready to move."

"Arun!" Donna screamed, as she saw him slip off the cable

and pitch sideways to dangle by his fingertips, 40 metres above the icy ground.

Instinct took over and Arun's hands tightened their grip while he hooked the crook of his right leg over the steel wire and brought his left leg up, too. He hung like a sloth, trying not to think about the drop below.

"Arun, are you OK?" Donna called across. She gripped the trailing coil of rope in her hands. "Should I pull you in? Wait, I'm coming out there." She went for the rungs of the hooped ladder.

"No!" Arun shouted. "I've got this."

His mind raced through his predicament. He couldn't stay in this position for much longer as his limbs were tiring, which meant he would have to try and get back on top of the wire. To do that, he would need to somehow swing back up, but how? And then it came to him - basic physics. To counter gravity, he would need to generate upward force and there was only one way to do that. Carefully, he unhooked his left leg and raised it to point his toes skywards. Then he swung it downwards and away from his body, pivoting his hips through a half-circle using the cable as an axis, while twisting his frame. His down-swinging leg acted as a counterweight, shifting his hips back on top of the steel rope.

"Yessss!" Donna said, punching the air with her free hand.

"Ouch," Arun said. "I think I crushed something. I'm going to be so bruised in the morning."

"Not as much as if you fell. You're doing great, Arun. You're a natural. Like a real monkey!" Donna said.

"Why is it even when you think you're being encouraging, you're still giving me abuse?" Arun muttered to himself.

Now back on top of the wire, he resumed pulling himself along the final few metres towards the stranded cable car.

"It's going to fall!" Sam shrieked, watching the stricken lodge begin to slide over the cliff. "Grab it, quick!"

MANDROID crossed the space in two strides and launched itself full length at the toppling chalet, like a cricketer diving for a catch.

KRRUNCHH!

It locked its hands on the rear of the building, clamping its fingers into the wood. The back of the building continued to lift but MANDROID pushed downwards, adding its weight to the near end of the see-sawing building.

Sam watched through his fingers while the wooden

structure creaked and groaned, before it settled once more.

"I was afraid it was going to break in half," Sam said, the colour drained from his face.

My scans determined that the lower half of the building had been equipped with steel beams for additional strength. It will hold together but not for long.

"And then?"

Total collapse.

"How long is not long?"

Two hundred and eighty-seven seconds.

Sam made a pained expression. "Next time, just say around five minutes. What are we going to do? If we move, the building goes; if we stay, it breaks up and goes anyway. Can we get the people out?"

Negative. The rear doors are blocked by the avalanche flow. The only open exit points are at the front.

"I need to think of something fast."

In the freight wagon, Moss was sitting on the floor, leaning against a crate. Sunny was reading her magazine, while Mertens continued to meditate.

Suddenly, Moss jumped up and sprang to his feet. "Did you feel that?" he said.

Sunny glanced up and listened to a faint rumbling sound.

Mertens opened his eyes. "It's the engine. The train is starting up." He uncrossed his legs and jerked his head to one side to crack his neck.

"That must mean the tunnel is clear," Moss said, rising to his feet. "We could be getting out of here?"

"Don't be so daft," Sunny said. "Why would they go to all this trouble to stop the train, take out the security detail and then let it just carry on with its journey? Something's wrong here."

"What do you think is happening?" Mertens said, standing up.

"This whole operation is about stealing this gold," Sunny said, gesturing at the crates. "So whatever's been happening outside while we've been waiting in here must be related to that. If this train is starting to move again, it must be because they're ready to come and take the gold."

"We have to stop them," Moss said.

"You're a lot more clever than you seem," Mertens said to Sunny, nodding his approval. "Yes, I agree. We need to be ready to defend this carriage. We can't let them get away with this."

Three carriages further along, in the passenger car behind the engine, Friedrich stiffened at the thrum of the engine. She was in complete darkness, due to the hood over her head. As she listened, she heard the crackle of a radio, the clump of boots and the click of the door opening and closing.

"Schäplitz? Buhringer?" she said. "Report."

"I hear you," Buhringer said from under his hood.

"Me, too," Schäplitz said.

"That's the sound of the engine running," Friedrich said. "Enough sitting around. We need to do something."

"How?" Buhringer said. "You heard them. There are explosives in this carriage. If we do anything..."

"It has to be a bluff," Friedrich said. "I heard the guard leave and if another one was in here, he'd have stopped us speaking. Besides, if they're going to move the train, they can't blow up a carriage."

"What do you want to do?"

"Get out of these restraints and see if we can stop this stupid train."

"Sounds like a plan," Schäplitz said. "And how do we do that?"

"You'll see."

* * *

Savitch's team of mercenaries – his explosives experts, foot soldiers, train engineers and communications specialists – took their seats on the train, filling up the remaining two passenger cars.

Drago, in the driver's seat, waited for his walkie-talkie to buzz. "Yes?" he said into it.

"Proceed," Savitch said, over the radio.

Drago turned the handle to start the train moving towards the now-cleared western portal, taking it back the way it had originally come.

13:28

Watched by the faces pressed against the steamed-up cable-car windows, Arun hauled himself the final metres. His ribs, ankle and hips were sore, having been in contact with the wire for most of the crawl, but the difficult part was still to come. He reached the clamp fixing the curved hanger arm to the cable. Below, the cabin rocked, suspended from the hanger.

The tower creaked again, ominously. Arun slid off the cable, letting his arms take his weight and looked down to ensure his feet were lined up with the top of the swaying car. He watched the gentle swing from side to side, judged the equilibrium mid-point and let go.

His feet touched down on the roof – and shot out beneath him, as the flat soles of his school shoes met the icy surface. He slammed on to the canopy and slipped towards the edge as the cabin tilted. Scrabbling for a grip, he caught hold of the fixing for the hanger arm and dug his fingers into the small gap between the metal bar and the roof, while his legs dropped over the side.

"Arun!" Donna screamed, her heart in her mouth.

Legs dangling, Arun gritted his teeth and hung on with one hand. He put the fingers of his other hand in his mouth, bit down and pulled to remove the glove. Then he reached for his belt with his free hand, stuck his thumb through the gate of the carabiner to unlatch it and grabbed hold of the ice-axe handle. His grip on the roof was loosening as his fingers began to tire, but desperation and adrenalin kicked in. With a last surge of strength, he swung the axe, driving the pick into the metal covering of the cable car. His feet scrabbled until they found a grip on the window surround and he slowly heaved himself back up on to the roof.

Exhausted, he collapsed with his back against the hanger arm, waiting for his pounding heart rate to slow.

The support tower swayed again. "Arun, we gotta hustle!" Donna called to him, looking around anxiously.

"I know," Arun complained. He climbed to his knees, untied the rope around his waist and tied it securely to the base of the hanger arm. "Now you tie your end, as taut as you can," he shouted to Donna.

"What are you thinking?" she said. "I can't pull that thing over here."

"Trust me. You won't have to."

Donna looped her end of the rope around the thickest steel beam she could find, pulled with all her weight to draw it tight and finished with a secure knot.

"Ready!" she called to Arun. "Do what you gotta do."

Arun sprawled on his front, leaned over with the ice axe and motioned for the passengers inside to move away from the window. He swung the axe, stabbing the point into the toughened safety glass of the cabin. It punched through, creating a spider's web of cracks, but the glass held. He was about to swing the axe a second time when a boot from inside the cabin sent the pane tumbling to the snow far below.

A bearded face popped out and stared upwards. "*Du bist ein Kind?*" the man said.

"Um, no *sprechen sie Deutsche*," Arun tried. "I'm English."

"You came to help us?"

"Yes. You have to get out before this whole thing falls."

"That rope. It is to help us get to the tower?"

"That's the idea."

"I'll send my boy first. He will help you. Then the women and children."

"OK. Give me a minute." Arun took another length of rope, tied it to the base of the hanger and draped the other end in front of the window.

"Good thinking," the bearded dad said. He helped his teenage son up on to the edge of the window. The lad grabbed the rope and easily climbed up alongside Arun.

"I'm Toni," the boy said. "You?"

"Ginger," Arun said, cringing inside.

"What's the rope for?" Toni said, looking at the line strung along from the cable car to the support mast.

"To help you guys get to the tower. You put your feet on the rope and hold the wire cable with your hands. Walk sideways. It's a lot easier and more stable than trying to freehand it."

Toni nodded. "I'll help the others up from the cabin. You help them on to the ropes."

"OK. And my partner over there will help them down. Let's hurry."

Sam was in a quandary. MANDROID's weight was holding the chalet in place, preventing it from toppling, but it couldn't stay that way for long. However, if MANDROID moved, the building would fall.

"I have an idea," Sam said to MANDROID. "You haven't done it before, but I think it's possible, in theory, like when you turned into the tail of an aeroplane."

You are proposing a new configuration?

184

"Yeah, I suppose I am," Sam agreed. "Here's what we're going to do…"

Moments later, MANDROID rose to its feet, keeping a firm grip on the ski lodge. It took sideways steps towards the brink of the precipice, changing hands as it worked its way along the structure, until it stopped at the cliff edge, almost parallel to the tipping point. The chalet continued to teeter and creak.

A small crowd of bedraggled holidaymakers gathered to watch the rescue operation.

MANDROID then dropped to its knees and burrowed its head into the gap between the base of the building and the packed ice of the verge, positioning its shoulders so they were wedged against the underside, like Atlas holding up the world.

"Now for the new part," Sam said.

A ripple pulsed through the mechanical legs, and components rejigged their positions in its wake. In a blur of motion, fragments twisted, slid and interlocked into new shapes and sequences until a cone-shaped nozzle extended from the heel of each foot.

"Remember to start easy and build power as you go," Sam said.

Initiating limited launch.

185

Sam felt his skin prickle as goosebumps crawled over his arms. The hum of rising power filled his ears.

MANDROID locked its shoulders against the bottom of the ski lodge, braced itself, and – *FWWOOOMM!!* Twin jets of blue flame blasted from the turbine engines in each leg. The chalet shuddered and emitted a crunching, grinding noise.

"It's breaking up!" Sam cried.

Negative. Structural integrity is holding. The sound you are hearing is the base scraping against the ice.

Slowly, almost imperceptibly, the wooden building advanced back up the slope. MANDROID throttlcd up to increase power, heaving the mass on its shoulders, and pushing the lodge forwards, centimetre by centimetre. The rear of the chalet was jammed up against tons of snow from the avalanche but the side was able to pivot away from the drop.

"It's working!" Sam said. "Keep going. You're doing great!"

GGGNNNGGGRRRRRR!!

With a final burst of thrust, MANDROID heaved the lodge clear of the brink. It cut the engines, settled on its two feet and leaned down to rip open a side door. A stream of people – some numbed, some distressed, some relieved – spilled from the lodge, to be greeted by the crowd of

186

onlookers. One or two embraced, in emotional reunions.

"Yes!" Sam punched the air with both fists and sank back in his seat, drained and elated. "You did it, big fella," he said.

Correction, Captain. We *did it,* MANDROID said.

Less than a kilometre away, the intact half of the train was crawling towards the open western tunnel mouth. The engine hauled three passenger carriages and the freight wagon.

Drago kept the speed low to avoid any remaining debris on the tracks getting caught under the wheels. A derailment now would be disastrous, as the gold was about to be collected.

In the passenger carriage directly behind the locomotive, Friedrich wriggled her zip-tied wrists beneath her bottom while bringing her knees up to her chin. She slipped the cuffs under her boots so her hands were now in front. After wrestling the hood off her head, she blinked to clear her dazzled eyes.

"Buhringer? Schäplitz? Stand, so I can see you."

Her two colleagues stumbled to their feet, one in the next row, the other opposite the aisle.

"Stay there. I'll be with you in a moment." She reached for her belt, loosened the buckle and pulled it to release a concealed blade hidden behind the clasp. Swiftly, she flipped the stubby knife round and cut the plastic ties binding her wrists and ankles, and did the same for her teammates.

"Now we stop this train," she said.

13:37

Fire Chief Janssen watched sternly as the last flames from the burning train were extinguished by his fire crews. It had taken fifteen minutes to bring the conflagration under control, and that meant fifteen minutes in which he was unable to send help to the avalanche-struck resort.

He reached for his radio. "Thomas? What's the latest?"

"Those army choppers you requested are on their way, along with Mountain Rescue. They should be at the resort in around thirty minutes."

"Half an hour's no good to me. I need them there now."

In London, at the Intelligence Service headquarters, Quinn was pouring a large whisky from his hip flask into a mug. He was about to take a glug when he spied Burgess eyeing him disapprovingly from behind his monitor screen.

"What? I'm in the public sector, which means drinking at work is expected," Quinn growled.

"It isn't that," Burgess said.

"Then what? I don't need you looking at me with a face

like a smacked bottom."

"You don't have children, do you?" Burgess said.

"Is it that obvious?" Quinn looked at his own wobbly reflection in the cup.

"Try being … gentler with them. It gets better results."

Quinn's mouth twisted as if he were sucking a lemon slice soaked in vinegar. "I don't need you telling me how to—"

"Just try it. See what happens. If it doesn't work, go back to the Mr Angry routine. It won't kill you to be nice."

"And how do you know that?"

"Remember who needs who the most right now."

"Come on, you can do it. Almost there. You're doing great," Donna said, calling encouragement to the holidaymakers clambering across from the cable car, holding on to the steel wire while shuffling their feet along the rope.

Already, eight people had made their way across and were climbing down the central ladder to the safety of the ground, while the tower continued to sway and creak.

Donna reached out to help the next climber down from the rope. That meant there were five to go – three already on the rope – plus Arun.

At the gondola end, Toni helped his father use the short

length of line to reach the roof and Arun showed him where to position his hands and feet on the cables.

"You next," Arun said to the older teen.

Toni nodded. "Thank you for coming to help us. You're crazy, but I am grateful. How can we ever repay you for this?"

Arun smiled. "Seriously? You can forget we were ever here and tell that to the others, too."

"I can do that." Toni jumped up for the cable, did two chin-ups and began scuttling across.

Arun turned to view the western edge of the resort, shielding his eyes from the glare of the snow. He could make out the blue and gold of MANDROID, a crowd of spectators, and the chalet, still intact.

"*M-Mama! Hilf mir!*" a plaintive voice cried.

Arun whirled towards the sound and saw a child around eight years old clinging to the rope system, her body stiff and tears streaking her face. The girl was most of the way across and only a few metres from the tower platform, but had made the mistake of looking down and was now stricken with fear.

"It's OK, I'm right here," Donna coaxed, stretching out her hand, but the child screwed her eyes shut and shook her head fiercely.

GGNNNRRRRR!!

The tower groaned again and swayed further than it had before, stretching both the cable and the rope. This time it did not swing back.

Donna took one look and sprang into action, vaulting on to the handrail and reaching for the steel cable above.

"Hold on," she called. "I'm coming."

The full weight of the leaning pylon was now bearing on the wire and it was only a matter of seconds before the cable broke or slipped its mounting.

Donna swung hand over hand along the line, swiftly reaching the girl. She dropped her feet on to the rope and bent her knees to bring her face to the same height as the child's.

"I don't know if you can understand me," Donna said, "but we have to get the heck out of here fast. This whole thing's gonna fall."

Opening her eyes, the girl blinked in surprise to see Donna beside her.

"Hold on to me," Donna said. "I'll guide you back."

"*Huckepack!*" Toni shouted from further along.

The child nodded, smiled weakly and wrapped her arms around Donna's neck. She then brought her legs up and clamped them around Donna's waist.

"You're heavier than you look," Donna muttered, trying to avoid being strangled by the tightly gripping arms. With the girl now riding piggyback, Donna sidestepped along the rope, holding the wire for support. The tower leaned again and the cable juddered.

"Come on, come on, come on," Donna said under her breath, willing the platform to draw closer. She reached it and jumped down, sprawling breathless with the girl beside her. Three more adults climbed across and helped the child down the central ladder. That left Toni, who was on the rope, and Arun, still atop the cable car.

"Arun, you gotta hustle!" Donna screamed, an uncharacteristic note of panic in her voice.

Arun looked and his heart skipped when he saw the support tower begin to drift away from him as one of its legs buckled. The tower's shifting weight bore down on the rope, straining it beyond its limits, and it in turn pulled at the mounting on top of the cable car. Arun was about to jump for the wire when – *SNAPPP!!* The climbing rope broke and the two ends fell. Toni, who was most of the way across, clung to the steel cable, his legs dangling, and swung arm over arm to the safety of the tower.

On the ground and looking up, the huddle of rescued passengers saw everything: the collapsing tower, the endangered cable car, the now-stranded rescuer.

"*Schnell!*" one of them said, scrambling to unearth a partially buried backpack.

Arun had one priority, namely to get off the cable car before it, too, fell. He grabbed the ice axe, looped the strap several times around his wrist and leapt, hooking the axe pick on to the steel cable. Holding on with both hands, he kicked away from the cabin roof and let gravity take over, hanging from the ice pick and coasting down the wire as if it were a zipline.

Donna, meanwhile, clung to the central ladder, hooking her arms and legs through the rungs as the lattice tower began to topple in slow motion – taking the cable down with it.

Cold wind whipped through Arun's hair as he picked up speed, sliding down the cable. The tower platform was coming up at him fast and he realised he hadn't worked out how to stop without slamming into the metal frame. It ceased to matter when he felt the cable slip from its support, go slack and send him plummeting to the ground.

Watching out of the MANDROID cockpit window, Sam counted the people exiting the battered chalet building.

"…Forty-four … forty-five! That's everyone, right, MANDROID?"

That is correct. All survivors present and accounted for.

"Great. We should go check on Arun and Donna."

Before you do, my cameras have detected something you should be aware of, MANDROID said.

A live video feed flashed up on the window, displaying the throng of onlookers. While Sam watched, the picture zoomed in and magnified on several hands holding up smartphones, all aimed at MANDROID.

13:41

Everything came crashing down at once: the cable car, the support tower, the haul cable – and Arun.

Irreparably damaged by the avalanche, one of the pylon's four legs finally buckled, kinking into a right angle. Losing a quarter of its weight-bearing capacity, the rest of the mast duly followed, leaning over with a tremendous grinding of galvanised steel.

Clinging to the ladder with all her strength, Donna shut her eyes tightly and gritted her teeth. Seemingly in slow motion, the lattice tower folded in half, bowed down and rested its top gently on the ground in an upside-down V-shape.

As soon as the mast began to pull away and drop, the steel cable tore free from its wheeled assembly and flopped downwards. No longer supported, the cable car plummeted, slammed on to the packed snow and crumpled like a soda can.

Arun fell, seeing his legs float upwards, and knew he was about to land on his back after plunging 40 metres.

He had the presence of mind to try and cover his head with his arms for all the good that would do, before he hit something firm that yielded and snapped taut, pinging him back in the air a few metres, before catching him again.

A loud cheer went up, and a startled Arun sat up to find himself lying on the nylon sheeting of a large tent. All around him, having just let go of the tent fabric, were the adults he had helped to rescue from the cable car.

"It worked!" Toni said, extending his hand to help Arun up. "I wasn't sure the cloth was strong enough to take your weight."

"Oi! When you've finished gassing, how about me?" Donna shouted from the ladder, now lying at a 45-degree angle, some 15 metres above the ground, wrapped in a tangled bird's nest of steel beams.

Toni dragged the makeshift safety net over to Donna, while his father ruffled Arun's hair and then swallowed him up in a bear hug.

"Thank you," the bearded man said, then ran over to help his son catch Donna.

In the MANDROID cockpit, Sam's heart sank at the sight of the phones pointed in his direction.

"Whoa," Sam said. "Are they...?"

Yes, the cameras are operational. A reasonable conjecture would be that recording is taking place. I have blocked livestreaming attempts.

"Oh, crud. Is there any way we can stop them taking pictures?"

A localised electromagnetic pulse would disable all electronic devices within the immediate vicinity.

"Do it!" Sam said. "And then let's find the others."

Outside among the happy reunions and cries of relief, as survivors embraced each other in the shattered remains of the Kallstein resort, some holidaymakers had their phones trained on the blue and gold giant watching over them.

"*Ist es ein Außerirdischer?*" someone said.

"*Ich weiß nicht, aber – ACH!*" the speaker jumped when the screen of her phone sparked and cracked, giving off a faint burning smell.

All around the resort, a chorus of disappointed voices cursed in unison as every phone, watch and camera died at the same time.

MANDROID gave a cheery wave and stepped over the crowd, heading towards the cable-car system.

The train continued to crawl towards the western mouth of the tunnel.

"We have the engine in front, two passenger cars behind and then the freight wagon," Friedrich said to Schäplitz and Buhringer, as they huddled by the door of the carriage. "We have to assume that everyone Savitch has brought with him is behind us, so the only chance we have is to go forward, take out the driver and stop the train."

Schäplitz smoothed his moustache with his fingers and nodded. "And all we have is your belt knife."

"And this," Buhringer said, unclipping a fire extinguisher from its wall bracket.

Friedrich led the way. She opened the gangway door to be faced by the rear of the locomotive and a metal door.

"Dang it!" she said. "It only opens from the inside. Now what?"

"We draw him out," Schäplitz said. "Get ready."

He jumped up, caught the edge of the carriage roof and pulled himself up. Making as much noise as possible, Schäplitz stomped along the curved top of the train.

In the driver's cab below, Drago kept his grip on the

accelerator handle, keeping the speed low, and brought the train back out into the Alpine air. Five hundred metres ahead, the tracks were buried in the runoff from the avalanche but that was of no concern. He wasn't planning on going much further.

CLUMP-CLUMP-CLUMP!

Drago scowled at the sound of footsteps on the roof; none of his team would be out there, which meant... He drew his automatic pistol and blasted several rounds into the ceiling. The footsteps ran towards the back of the carriage.

Drago swore, released the handle and went for the door. Because his hand was no longer on the controls, the fail-safe system kicked in, cutting the power and applying the emergency brake.

While the train slowed to a stop, Drago ripped open the door, gun in hand and – *FFFSSSSSHHHHHH!!* – walked face first straight into a freezing blast of carbon dioxide. He stiffened, and in that moment of hesitation Friedrich launched herself at him, ramming her head into his midriff and wrapping her arms around the big man's waist. She drove forwards, forcing Drago off his feet and back into the cab. As he dropped, he tucked in his knees, rolled on to his back and kicked out with both legs, sending Friedrich flying. He sprang upright again and aimed his pistol at the advancing Buhringer, who instinctively raised the fire extinguisher for protection.

BLAMM! The bullet punctured the pressurised steel tank and a white cloud hissed into the narrow space. Drago levelled the handgun again, picking out Buhringer's shape in the haze. His finger began to tighten on the trigger but Friedrich slammed her cupped hands over his ears. Drago screamed in pain as the shock wave pounded his eardrums and he stooped, stunned and dizzy. Buhringer swung the extinguisher, clonking him once on the head and the big man stayed down.

"We've stopped again," Moss said, steadying himself at the sharp braking. "That was a bit sudden."

"Emergency brake?" Sunny said.

"I don't think it's anything," Mertens said.

"How do you know?" Moss said. "We start, we stop, we start, we stop again. At some point they're going to try and come in here so we need to know what's happening out there."

Mertens pursed his lips and nodded slowly. "OK. I'll go."

"No, you've been out already," Moss said. "Let me do it. I'll scout around and report back."

"You're not trained for this," Mertens insisted. "I am. I'll go."

"Oh, for goodness' sake," Sunny said. "How about I go?" She reached for the handwheel in the floor, to open the escape hatch, then stopped when she realised Mertens was aiming his Steyr assault rifle at her head.

13:48

Once the train had stopped, Major Savitch stood and slid open a slat in the wall to peep outside. A bar of sunlight fell upon his eyes and confirmed that the train had left the tunnel. Satisfied, he tapped his train engineer on the shoulder and led him down the gangway, past the seated mercenaries, to the back of the train.

Savitch opened the carriage door and a chill blast of wintry air rushed in. He paused to eye the sealed door to the freight wagon that faced him. So near to the gold, yet so far. The engineer squeezed past him, jumped down to the track and removed the hook and chain to uncouple the wagons. The Major nodded in approval and checked his watch. Soon he would be able to begin transporting the gold to his waiting buyer, get paid, and his part in the operation would be over.

"Arun!" Donna ran over to clamp her arms around his skinny frame and squeezed. "You had me worried there," she said. "When you fell…"

Embarrassed, Arun tried unsuccessfully to shrug out of her grip. "It's Ginger, remember?" he said.

"Oops." Donna released him, much to the amusement of the onlookers.

"It's OK," Toni said. "You were never here and we didn't see you."

A small child approached Arun with a shy smile and held out her hands, presenting him with three chocolate bars.

"Wow, thank you," Arun said. "Um, *danke*. We didn't bring lunch, so yeah. This is great."

"Well, look who's finally showed up, as soon as food appears," Donna said, shielding her eyes from the sun while lifting her head to see the approaching MANDROID.

The ground shook slightly as the 20-metre-tall figure marched towards them. The small crowd gawked and shrank back. It stooped, curled up, retracting its limbs and reconfigured to its motor-home shape. Opening the cockpit door, Sam leaned out and beckoned his friends.

"Come on," he said. "Time to go. Enough people have seen us already."

Arun extended his hand and Toni grasped it firmly. "Is that thing for real?" Toni said.

"Yeah, but it doesn't exist," Arun said. "Just like the rest of us. We were never here."

Toni laughed. "As if anyone would believe us!"

"I'm Posh, by the way," Donna said, striding past them. "It's been emotional." She climbed up into the cabin, grateful for the warmth.

Arun took one last look at the smashed cable car, the mangled support tower and the grateful faces of the survivors. His knew his father would be proud that his life's work was being put to good use, but he would never know.

"Hurry it up, will you?" Donna called to him. "We're starving!"

"This is Giselle Dallmann reporting live from the eastern portal of the Kallstein railway tunnel. Earlier today, a landslide blocked the tunnel mouth, trapping a freight train inside. While recovery operations were underway, it is believed that an avalanche struck the nearby ski resort on the western side. I am with Fire Chief Norbert Janssen, who is coordinating rescue operations. Can you please provide an update?"

"As you can see, the situation is largely under control on this side," Janssen said, gesturing towards the open tunnel. "My concern is the ski resort, where we have lost contact and it is likely there are multiple casualties and people buried. We are unable to reach them because the avalanche has blocked the roads on that side. Army helicopters are on the way."

"Thank you, Chief Janssen. So, dramatic developments in the Alps today. Stay tuned for further bulletins on this breaking story as developments, uh, develop. This is Giselle Dallmann reporting." She pulled a face. "I really messed up the ending there."

"It's OK. The studio can cut that if they don't like it," her camera operator said.

"You've got a signal?" Janssen said.

"I do now," Giselle replied. "It's very strange. Since about twelve thirty, nothing worked, except for your radio. I had no mobile, no satellite. Like you said, we were being blocked by your mystery friend. Then about an hour ago it all came back online."

Janssen cocked his head, listening to a faint drumming sound, growing louder. "You might want to switch that camera back on and get a good shot of this."

The thudding noise grew louder until a massive twin-engine, six-rotor helicopter swooped overhead and roared westwards.

"That's not the army!" Janssen said. "What's it doing here?"

The Russian-built Mil Mi-26 heavy-transport helicopter thundered past, heading towards the other end of the tunnel.

"Move away from the hatch, Ms Patel," Mertens said, his hand steady on the assault rifle.

"I knew it!" Moss said. "As soon as you came back and said the others had been captured. You betrayed them. Your own teammates."

"Give yourself a pat on the back," Mertens said. "Patel, I want you to place your weapon on the floor, slowly. Then slide it over to me."

Sunny took out her borrowed Glock pistol and scooted it over to Mertens. "And to think I was starting to like you," she said.

"Now you, Moss," Mertens said. "Give me your gun."

Moss took a step to the side, aware that a crate stood between him and the Jagdkommando, restricting the sightlines. He unslung the P90 sub-machine gun from his shoulder, holding it high in his right hand while his left, hidden by his body, reached around to the waistband at the small of his back.

"Here. Safety's on. What's German for 'catch'?" Moss lobbed the gun to Mertens, who reached out his free hand to catch it.

In that split second of distraction, Moss dived to the floor and fired a shot from his Glock pistol.

Sunny flung herself down behind the nearest crate as a burst of automatic fire resounded off the walls.

"This is absurd," Mertens said. "You want to play hide and seek – in here? There is nowhere to hide."

Sunny and Moss both stayed low and said nothing, knowing that if they did they would give their locations away.

"As you wish." Mertens chambered a round. "Three … two … one … here I come."

In the train driver's cab, Friedrich grabbed Drago's automatic pistol. Looking out of the front window, she saw a bank of snow in front, burying the tracks. It had to have come from the ski slopes so she knew that following the drift uphill would lead to the resort.

Schäplitz watched her and voiced his thoughts. "You're thinking we should go and get help?"

Friedrich nodded. "But I don't want to leave our people behind in the first car, plus Savitch and his pigs are in the next two."

"Which means we are outnumbered, outgunned and

they have hostages," Buhringer said. "Evasion is the only choice we have."

Friedrich held up her hand for silence. "You hear that?" she said.

"What is it?" Schäplitz said, listening to the faint pounding sound, growing louder.

"Trouble," Friedrich said, moving for the door.

13:53

Back in the warm and familiar surroundings of the MANDROID motor home, Arun was handing out the chocolate bars.

"You should have seen it," Sam said, eyes bright with excitement. "It was like Iron Man with both thrusters firing and we pushed the whole building back up. Do you know how much horsepower we'd have needed?"

"What I want to know is why you got to sit in here while we had to freeze our butts off out there," Donna said. "You have no idea how terrifying that was, although only Arun got scared. I had a collapsing tower around me, and Arun fell all the way."

Captain Evans was selected for his creative thinking, MANDROID said.

"Ah, you made him say that," Donna said.

"No, I didn't," Sam said, taking the bait. "He can't lie."

Donna cocked an eyebrow. "Since when? Hey, Mandy, can you lie? Does your programming allow that?"

If it did, it would be remiss of me to admit it.

"Hah! Knew it," Donna said.

"Ooh, look what else I found," Arun said, rummaging through the salvaged climber's backpack. He held up two granola bars.

"I ain't eating that rabbit food," Donna said.

"See?" Sam said. "You shouldn't have made me clean up all that stuff. I'm sure there were some Pringles left in one of those tubes."

"I'm sure there weren't," Donna said.

"More for me, then, if you don't want any," Arun said, tearing open a wrapper. "We need to make a list of things we need for next time, if there is a next time. I'm thinking food, comms..."

"Proper uniforms," Sam said.

"Guns," Donna added.

I have an incoming communication, MANDROID said.

"Uh-oh," Donna, Sam and Arun said at the same time.

Quinn's face flashed up on the windscreen.

"Hello, kids," he said, forcing a smile.

"Eww, what's he doing? That's so weird," Donna said under her breath.

"I'm delighted to see you've returned to stealth mode once more and are not walking around outside."

"We had to go out," Arun said. "To help people."

"So I've been told. I need to ask you something."

"Sure."

"Do you recall why I sent you out to Austria in the first place?"

"To pick up two of your agents, trapped on a train?"

Quinn scratched his stubbly chin. "Yes. And how is that going, given it's the only reason you're there?"

"Oh, we forgot about them," Sam said. "They must still be in the tunnel."

Quinn willed himself not to explode. "Well, if it isn't too much trouble, would you be so kind as to go and pick them up for me and bring them home?"

"Yeah, we can do that," Donna said.

"Let me know when you have them. Old Spice out."

"Y'know, I think I preferred him when he was screaming at us," Arun said, taking a bite of his cereal bar. "You sure you don't want any? It's really good."

"Go on, then," Sam said, holding out his hand. "I'm hungry enough."

Friedrich stood in the doorway of the train and listened to the percussive thumping sounds of the approaching helicopter.

"That's not one of ours," she said. "It's way too big."

Buhringer spotted it first and pointed. "You're right. That's a Mil Mi-26 heavy transport. What's that doing here?"

"And what's it dragging?" Schäplitz said, pointing to a thick metal disc, dangling from a heavy chain beneath, like an enormous bath plug.

"You have eight crates to hide behind, positioned in twos," Mertens said in the freight wagon, assault rifle at the ready. "That means I will find you very quickly. Why not surrender now and save me the trouble?"

Moss knew he was right. There was no place to hide and it was only a matter of time before Mertens caught him or Sunny.

"OK," Moss said, crouching low. "If I give myself up, will you let Sunny go?"

"Andy, no!" Sunny said from her position.

"This is very touching and romantic," Mertens said, homing in on the voices, "but no one is leaving. You both know too much."

Outside, the giant 40-metre-long helicopter slowed and hovered directly above the freight carriage. It began to gradually lower itself, lining up the hanging metal disc with the dead centre of the rail wagon's roof.

Savitch held his cap in place as he stood on the step outside the passenger carriage and watched the descending helicopter whipping up dust and stone fragments.

Friedrich pulled herself up on to the roof of the engine for a better view of the proceedings. She could see the curved roofs of three carriages before her and the tunnel mouth behind. The thudding sound of the helicopter hammered the air, and the metal disc it was carrying closed the gap to the freight-car roof.

Whipping out the pistol she had taken from Drago, she gripped it in both hands, closed one eye and took careful aim before opening fire. *BLAM-BLAM-BLAM!*

Savitch's smile of satisfaction vanished at the sight of bullet holes spiderwebbing across the cockpit window of the helicopter. Immediately, the chopper banked as the pilot spun the aircraft away from the incoming fire. The hanging disc clunked against the roof, now off-centre, and locked in place.

Savitch roared in anger, jumped for the carriage edge and pulled himself up to see over the roof. *PTOWWW!* A bullet pinged close to his head and he dropped down again.

Flinging open the door, he roared at his team, sitting comfortably in their seats. "There's a commando on the roof of the engine! Get her!"

13:58

"Urgh. This tastes like cardboard," Sam complained, chewing on the cereal bar in the MANDROID camper van.

"Told you," Donna said.

"I like it," Arun said with a shrug.

Donna cleared her throat loudly, for effect. "As I was saying, we have to get to that train, find those two agents and we're done here, is that right?"

"Yeah, I guess," Sam said.

"OK. Let's get over there. MANDROID, do your thing."

Affirmative, Admiral. Please take your seats.

"I missed!" Friedrich said, crouching on the roof of the engine. "I had a clear shot at that pig!"

"Forget about it," Schäplitz called up to her. "We've got to move."

He leapt from the carriage step on to the snowy overspill with Buhringer close behind and they raced uphill away from the rail tracks.

The passenger carriage door opened and armed soldiers

spilled out. Friedrich took one look, pelted down the length of the train roof while bullets sliced the air around her, and launched herself off to land on the nearest snowbank. Scrambling to her feet, she charged up the slope, slipping and sliding, with Savitch's men in close pursuit.

At the same time, the massive helicopter lifted upwards, its twin turboshaft engines roaring. The suspended chain drew taut and the freight wagon slowly rose into the air, swinging at an alarming 30-degree angle since the electromagnet had been positioned off-centre after Friedrich had fired at the chopper.

Seconds earlier, inside the freight car, Mertens had been closing in on his quarry. He knew from their voices that Moss was behind a crate at the far end and Sunny was behind the crate in front of him. But Moss was armed, which made him the greater threat and, therefore, the one to be neutralised first.

Mertens crept closer, planting his feet squarely and moving with silent, ninja-like menace. His finger remained on the trigger of his assault rifle.

KLUNKK! A heavy object slammed down on the roof of the wagon, solidly enough to shake the walls. Sunny looked at the ceiling in alarm, half expecting it to cave in.

Moss, meanwhile, was coiled like a spring, ready to fling himself aside as soon as Mertens appeared. If he was lucky, he might get a shot off from the Glock, but it would only be as a distraction; the chance of hitting a target under these circumstances was virtually nil.

Mertens rounded a corner and caught sight of Moss's heel poking out from behind a crate. He smiled. It would be easier to kill Moss if he winged him first. He took aim and his finger tightened on the trigger.

Suddenly, the floor lurched upwards, tipping lengthways. Mertens, in mid-stride, was flung off balance and tumbled down the slope. Moss, who was already on all fours, sprawled flat, while Sunny was bashed against the door.

Bullets ripped into the snow, exploding all around Buhringer, Friedrich and Schäplitz as they sprinted up the snowbank towards the resort. Savitch's men were right behind.

The three Jagdkommando soldiers reached the top of the slope and dived over it – only to stop short in amazement at the blue and gold metal giant striding towards them.

"Are those our guys?" Donna asked, zooming in on her console screen for a better look.

Negative. Uniforms denote Austrian Special Forces operatives, MANDROID replied.

"We're looking for two people, not three, and Mr Quinn said we'd know them when we see them," Arun said.

"And who are those people chasing them?" Sam said, pointing as Savitch's troops crested the hill and also stopped at the sight of MANDROID. "They don't have army uniforms."

"Can I have a weapons scan, please?" Arun said. "What are we dealing with?"

The Jagdkommando are unarmed. Their pursuers are equipped with Steyr assault rifles, Glock pistols, explosive devices and hand-to-hand combat weapons, MANDROID replied.

"That's not a fair fight," Donna said. "Can we even it up a bit?"

Savitch's troops stared warily at the colourful automaton towering over them, and lowered their sights to the three Jagdkommando who huddled in its shadow.

"Lay down your weapons or there will be …

consequences," a harsh, metallic voice boomed in perfect German. "You have ten seconds to comply."

The soldiers looked at each other uneasily before a dozen of them raised their assault rifles to take aim at the MANDROID cockpit windows.

"Hah! Those aren't guns," the metal giant said. "Now, these ... these are guns."

Hatches opened in the robotic arms, panels slid aside and a pair of enormous rotary auto-cannon slid into view and locked.

Savitch's troops quailed at the sight.

"Oh, and I have these puppies, too." A chest plate opened and the tips of six air-to-ground missiles gleamed in the sunshine.

Assault rifles and handguns clattered on to the frozen snow.

"Awww, you guys are no fun."

Savitch stood in the doorway of the passenger carriage and scowled while watching the enormous Mil Mi-26 helicopter head south down the mountainside, with the skewed freight wagon swinging beneath. The electromagnet was holding but it could easily slip because of the sharp angle, and then the cargo would be lost.

He ducked back inside the car where the battered Drago was waiting.

"I am sorry, Major. I failed you," Drago said, looking sheepish.

Savitch eyed the egg-sized lump on the taller man's head. "It was three against one," he said. "I don't expect you to win every fight. Besides, it hasn't affected the plan. Are you able to complete the mission?"

"I am, Major. I won't fail you again." Drago gave a salute.

Savitch nodded. "I know you won't." He drew his pistol and – *BLAMM!* – Drago's body hit the carriage floor.

The Major turned and addressed his dozen remaining troops. "Time to go!" he barked. He unzipped his black jacket, turned it inside out and pulled it on again to display the markings of a Jagdkommando Special Forces operative. He opened the door and jumped down beside the tracks.

His soldiers did the same, reversing their jackets, and followed him up the snowbank, towards the Kallstein resort.

14:08

Sunny's stomach lurched as the freight wagon spun and swayed beneath the transport helicopter. Being at the bottom end of the sloping floor with the door behind her, she struggled to find her feet.

Crumpled next to her was Mertens, also trying to untangle his limbs. His assault rifle rested between the two of them.

At the other end of the car, Moss sprawled flat, trying not to slide head first down the incline.

Sunny flailed her arm towards the gun. She missed the barrel but her fingers closed on the webbing of the shoulder strap. Mertens stretched and grabbed the stock. It was now a tug of war.

"Andy!" Sunny screamed. "Could do with a hand here!"

Moss wobbled unsteadily to his knees. He couldn't see clearly because crates were in the way, but from her voice he could tell that Sunny was behind the crate on the right, which meant Mertens was likely to be behind the one on the left.

"Hang on!" he yelled, rising to his feet and stumbling forwards.

Mertens twisted to close his other hand on the rifle butt and heaved with his full strength. Sunny, who had looped the strap around her wrist, felt herself dragged across the floor towards him.

"Let go!" Mertens aimed a vicious kick in Sunny's direction, connecting with her ribs. She cried out in pain and released her grip.

Mertens pushed himself upright, leaning his back against the wall for support, and aimed the gun at the onrushing Moss.

Moss ducked down, lowered his head and slammed shoulder first into the crate, throwing his full weight and momentum against it. Ordinarily, the crate would never have budged but with the slope of the floor and the swing of the carriage, his charge drove it off its pallet and it slid towards Mertens, flattening him against the wall with a sickening crunch. The assault rifle fell from his limp hand.

"Quick, before they change their minds," Friedrich said, grabbing a sub-machine gun from the pile of surrendered weapons and motioning for Buhringer and Schäplitz to do the same.

"Get on your knees with your hands behind your heads," Schäplitz ordered, brandishing his weapon.

Savitch's men reluctantly dropped to the snow.

"What was that all about?" Sam said, watching the surrender on screen from inside MANDROID.

"I'm sure we'll find out later," Arun said. "We should get to that train and find Mr Quinn's missing agents."

Attention. I detect incoming aircraft, MANDROID said.

"What kind?" Donna said.

Radio intercepts indicate eighteen Austrian Air Force helicopters are in flight, plus four Mountain Rescue helicopters. ETA is approximately one minute.

"And we can't be seen," Arun said. "Let's get to that train quickly while they deal with the mess here."

Buhringer looked up as the shadow of MANDROID fell over him. The giant figure stepped over the cowering forms of Savitch's soldiers and stomped off down the mountain slope towards the railway line.

"What was that all about?" he said in bemusement.

"I'm sure we'll find out later," Friedrich said.

"I hear choppers," Schäplitz said. "Finally, some backup arrives."

Led by brightly coloured Mountain Rescue Airbus H145s, the army helicopters, a mix of Bell Twin Hueys and S-70 Black Hawks, thundered overhead and fanned out in search of suitable landing sites.

They were watched by bedraggled crowds of avalanche survivors who waved and whooped with relief.

The first choppers touched down and medics dashed across the frozen surface to be mobbed by the throng.

Another helicopter landed beside the three Jagdkommando and their prisoners, its rotors whipping up swirls of snow. Troopers hit the ground and ran over. Their team leader saluted.

"Corporal Friedrich, it's good to see you again," he said. "What is your situation?"

Friedrich waved her sub-machine gun in the direction of Savitch's mercenaries. "We have a war criminal on the loose. All of these are enemy combatants. Round them up and keep an eye on them."

"Yes, ma'am."

"And find me some more soldiers. I have two teams down and more enemy hostiles in the vicinity."

The trooper hesitated. "Corporal, one of our spotters says he saw a blue and gold vehicle further down. Should we engage?"

"No," Friedrich said. "It's one of ours." She paused and looked down towards the train tracks, her brow furrowed in thought. "You guys can take it from here?" she said to her colleagues, who nodded in reply. "OK. Send me backup, as soon as you can."

"Where are you going?" Buhringer said.

"After Savitch. That monster isn't getting away." Friedrich broke into a run and headed downhill.

Savitch stood atop a steep drift and waved both arms in the air. One of the remaining airborne helicopters drew closer and touched down nearby.

Its side doors slid open and a hand beckoned. "You're right on time, Major," the co-pilot said.

"So are you," Savitch said. "Let's go while we can."

"What about the others?" the co-pilot said. "I was expecting more of you."

"What about them?" Savitch climbed into the chopper. "They knew the rendezvous. I have a schedule to maintain."

Once those of Savitch's troops who'd made it were on board, the Black Hawk lifted into the air and headed south, along the same flight path as the huge Mil Mi-26.

Seconds later, Friedrich mounted the snowbank, her breath puffing in white clouds. She stared as the chopper wheeled away, dropped to her knees in defeat and then swore.

"No, no, no." She punched the snow in frustration, which is when a sparkling object caught her eye.

14:15

"MANDROID, we're going to need scans of the train, please," Arun said from inside the humanoid-shaped vehicle crouching beside the train.

Scanning now, MANDROID replied.

"It's not much of a train, is it?" Donna said. "I mean, an engine and three cars? Where's the rest of it?"

Emerald-green 3D wireframe models of the train carriages appeared on the head-up windscreen display. Seated people appeared in red outline.

The locomotive and last two passenger cars are empty. However, I detect thirty people in the first carriage, all unconscious.

"Anyone we know?" Sam said.

Negative. I detect no familiar biosignals.

"This makes no sense," Arun said. "Where are the people we're meant to pick up?"

"I'll tell you what makes even less sense," Sam said. "We went to all that trouble to clear the other end of the tunnel but the train came out of this side. Why would it do that?"

"Maybe she knows," Donna said, looking at her screen. "We should ask her."

"Ask who?"

"That soldier down there. She's waving at us."

Sam zoomed in and displayed Friedrich's image on the cockpit display.

"MANDROID, can you tell us what she's saying?" Arun said.

Amplifying the audio now...

"*Savitch hat den Zug genommen!*" Friedrich shouted, her voice filling the cabin. "*Sie gingen in diese Richtung!*" She pointed south.

"She seems excited about something," Sam said. "MANDROID, translate, please."

The Special Forces Corporal is saying someone took the train.

"Well, duh. What else are you gonna do with it?" Donna said.

No, she is saying someone named Savitch took the train – by which she means they stole it and went south.

"What? They picked it up and walked off with it?"

Flew, to be precise.

"They flew off with it?" Donna repeated.

Yes.

"And we're sitting here talking?" Donna rolled her eyes. "What's wrong with this picture? MANDROID, flight mode."

"Can we track it?" Arun said.

Negative. However, there is an Austrian Air Force helicopter moving in that direction.

"OK. Follow it, then. Let's go!"

Friedrich watched as the metal giant stepped back from the locomotive and moved to the clear area in front of the train. It seemed to stumble and fall but tucked in its arms and flattened as it dropped. Parts shuffled and realigned as smoothly as flowing liquid. A pair of tail fins emerged and rocket engines fired from beneath, lifting it into the air. It hovered for a moment, banked south and disappeared with a thunderous roar.

Watching it depart in disbelief, Friedrich shook her head and said to herself, "That is not going into my debriefing report."

Moss crawled over to where Sunny leaned against the wall, nursing her bruised side.

"How are you feeling?" he asked.

"It's not as bad as getting shot," she said, wincing as she

felt her ribs. "Luckily, nothing's broken."

Moss sat next to her. "You realise we're airborne, right?"

Sunny shot a glowering look at him. "It doesn't take a former detective to work that out."

"So what do we do?"

"I'd say opening the hatch and jumping out isn't on the cards, so what *can* we do? Wait until they put it down and come knocking for the gold?"

"That's not going to work. As long as we were by the train, we knew what we were dealing with. Now they could drop this in a field, rig explosives on the doors and we'd be dead meat."

"Which means we have to get out before they land this."

Moss nodded. "Guess I'll have to open the hatch, to see where we are."

He lay front down on the floor and began crawling up the sloping, swaying floor.

Quinn chewed on a stubborn hangnail. He had a nub of skin between his teeth and wavered, unsure if he should pull or just snip with his incisors. He decided to pull and promptly regretted it as he felt the sharp pain of a tear followed by oozing blood. He swore and got up, wandering over to where Burgess sat, listening in to chatter.

"What's the latest?" Quinn said.

Burgess removed the headphones, sat back and stretched. "Well, the good news is that Mountain Rescue and the Austrian army are all over the scene. Somewhat miraculously, everyone caught in the avalanche made it out alive. Those buried were dug out well before the emergency services got there."

"Who'd have thought it, eh?" Quinn chewed his lip. "Any word from those brats?"

"That's the bad news."

"For heaven's sake, how long does it take to find two people on board a train? It's been twenty minutes. Get them on the line."

"With all due respect, sir, no."

Quinn reacted as if he'd been slapped. "What?" A vein bulged dangerously on his forehead. "You work for me, son, so you do what I say."

Burgess placed his hands behind his head. "Uh, technically no. I'm still on probation, so you can fire me if you want, in which case I'll pack up and leave right now."

Quinn narrowed his eyes. "Good point, well made. Go on."

"You told the kids to let you know when they found your agents. They haven't called because they haven't found them. If you keep harassing them it's only going to cause them more stress and will waste valuable time."

"But … but … I *want* to harass them. It makes me feel better. Gives me a sense of control." Quinn's mobile rang. It was C, his boss. "Yes?" he answered.

"It's been over an hour," C said. "Has your *S.T.E.A.L.T.H.* playgroup completed their mission yet?"

Quinn paused. "Yes, sir. They're on their way back, even as we speak."

"Oh? That's … very good. I'll expect a full report and debrief by close of play today."

"Yes, sir." Quinn ended the call.

Burgess smiled at him. "How did it feel, being put under extra pressure while trying to do your job. Did you like it?"

"Of course I didn't like it," Quinn snapped.

"That's what I was trying to say to you about the kids." Burgess picked up the headphones again. "And you just lied to your boss."

"I'm a spy," Quinn said. "It's my job. He should expect it." He glanced at the clock on the wall. "Now, don't let me down, kids," he said under his breath, "or we're all finished."

14:22

"This is ridiculous!" Moss spluttered. He slid down the skewed floor of the freight wagon once again. "Every time I get halfway, it swings or it dips or it jolts or it sways and – argh."

"You need a rope or something," Sunny said, sitting back against the wall.

"We don't have any," Moss said, breathing hard from the exertion. "And if we did, there's nothing to tie it to."

Sunny ignored her aching ribs and put her mind to the task. "What we need is something that will improve your grip while climbing a steep slope, like wearing crampons or using an ice axe... Wait, I've got it."

She sidled over to the crate pinning Mertens against the wall. There was a small gap in which he was squished.

"Oh, this is going to be so gross," Sunny said, reaching into the space. She found a trousered leg and worked her way down the calf to the boot. Fumbling around, her fingers closed on the hilt of a boot knife. She drew it and held it out. "This might work."

Moss nodded and reached for the short, stubby blade, but Sunny ignored him. "I'll do it," she said. "You're tired and I'm more supple." She hefted the dagger before reversing her grip and stabbing it into the wooden floor. It bit deeply and Sunny began to haul herself upwards, in the direction of the hatch.

Three kilometres behind the giant Mil Mi-26 helicopter flew the Black Hawk carrying Savitch and his remaining troops.

"Where are we going?" the pilot asked Savitch, shouting above the noise of the turbines.

"About forty kilometres south-east, to Lake Zell," Savitch replied. "You can drop us there."

"Sure. Anything to help our brave Special Forces. I'm a big fan, you know. You guys are the best."

"I don't find you amusing," Savitch said, stony-faced.

The pilot took the hint and kept quiet.

Following at a discreet distance, the MANDROID plane flew low, skimming the tree-lined tops of mountains and hills.

"Wow, it's so pretty out here," Donna said, watching the view from several screens on the horseshoe-shaped console around her. "So green and open."

"MANDROID, can you scan that helicopter in front?" Arun said.

It is an Austrian army Sikorsky S-70A-42 utility helicopter, fully laden with fourteen personnel on board, including pilots.

"Yet it's leaving a disaster area with over a hundred people needing help. That's not at all suspicious, is it? I wonder where it's going."

"Are you sure they can't see us?" Sam asked.

I am maintaining a course directly behind. The only way an observer could positively identify this craft would be if they turned the helicopter around.

"And if they did that, we'd turn, too, to stay on their blind side?"

Affirmative.

"What I still don't get is why you'd steal a train and fly off with it," Donna said. "Is it made of gold or something?"

"Just hold this course, MANDROID, and stay out of sight," Arun said.

Sunny drove the blade into the floor again, trying to ignore the ache in her ribs while straining to pull herself up the last few centimetres to reach the recessed escape hatch.

"Made it," she called down to Moss, and reached into the

hollow for the handwheel. She spun it to unlock, heaved it upwards and latched it in the open position. A blast of fresh, frigid air whooshed into the carriage and Sunny peered down through the open hatch to see bare hills, mountain pastures and conifers whizzing below at 200 kilometres an hour.

"Hold on," Moss said. He removed the belt from his trousers and lobbed it in Sunny's direction. She caught it by the buckle and let the loose end hang down.

Moss began crawling up the sloping floor again, stretched out his hand, and closed it on the dangling belt strap. With Sunny taking the strain, he hauled his way up until he drew alongside her.

"Where are we?" he asked.

"See for yourself," Sunny said, her face illuminated by the daylight streaming in and hair fluttering in the breeze.

Moss glanced for a second through the open hatch and immediately ducked back into the wagon, a look of stark terror across his face. "Oh, my gosh, oh, my gosh, oh, my gosh," he babbled.

"Andy! What's wrong?" Sunny said, alarmed.

Cold drops of sweat beaded Moss's forehead and his breath came in short gasps. His eyes were tightly closed and his teeth clamped together.

"Andy! I'm here," Sunny said from beside him. "What's wrong?"

Moss shook his head and kept his eyes tightly shut.

"Andy, I get it," Sunny said, as realisation dawned. "Listen to my voice. I want you to breathe in deeply, hold it for a few seconds and then breathe out. Come on, do it with me. Breathe in, deep as you can. I'll count to five."

Trembling, Moss took a breath, held it and released.

"Good," Sunny said. "Now again, let's breathe together."

She continued to gently coax him until he stopped hyperventilating and his galloping pulse slowed down once more.

"That's right," Sunny said. "You're doing really well. Breathe with me. It's OK."

Moss's eyes blinked open. He gasped and let out a sob. "I'm sorry."

Sunny watched him with concern. "It's all good. You just had a panic attack, that's all."

"I couldn't breathe. I thought I was going to faint, or die."

Sunny stroked his face. "You were nearly thrown out of an aeroplane not so long ago, and you survived a plane crash. I'd be surprised if you *didn't* have PTSD after that."

"I'm sorry. I'm useless."

"Don't be silly. You got to this hatch, didn't you? At some

point, we're going to have to jump. Do you think you can manage that?"

Moss swallowed hard and nodded.

"Good, because I really don't want to have to push you out."

The Mil Mi-26 helicopter continued its eastward course, with its unusual cargo dangling beneath.

14:28

"Hey, look," Sam said. "Up in front."

Arun looked up from the data screen he was reading and Donna tore her eyes away from the Alpine landscapes.

"What is it?" Arun said, only half focusing.

"I think I can see the train. That Black Hawk we've been following has been catching up and I think that's it." Sam pointed in the direction of the cockpit window, from his rear seat.

"MANDROID, can you zoom in on that object, please?" Arun said.

A magnified image of the enormous six-rotored Mil Mi-26 transport helicopter with the freight wagon suspended beneath flashed up on the window display.

"Hm," Donna said. "That's one way to do it. Can you do a scan? See what's on board?"

Negative, not from this range, but the Mil Mi-26 helicopter is slowing and descending, MANDROID reported.

"It's landing?" Arun said. "Great. Time to find those agents."

"We're dropping height, and we just went over a road," Sunny said to Moss. She lay on her front, watching the terrain passing below through the open escape hatch.

Moss rested beside her but stayed on his back, eyes fixed on the ceiling and refusing to look down.

"Once we get low enough, we're going to have to jump, OK?" Sunny said. "Close your eyes if you have to."

"I'm ready," Moss said, although he didn't look it.

The Black Hawk helicopter clattered past the Mil Mi-26 and roared towards a pristine Alpine lake, covering over five square kilometres. The chopper dropped low, skimming the lake's surface, and came to land in a meadow close to the water's edge.

Savitch jumped out and led the way, closely followed by his troops. They crossed the field, cut through a clump of trees and stopped by a small staging area, where two boxy lorries were parked, along with two SUVs, each towing a jet ski on a trailer, and a small group of men, some zipping up wetsuits. A pair of 13-metre-long centre-console boats bobbed nearby.

The men all stood to attention and saluted smartly upon Savitch's arrival.

"Welcome, Major. Everything is ready," one of the drivers said.

"Excellent," Savitch said. "Let's finish this."

The Black Hawk helicopter rose into the air and was gone.

Watching through the open hatch of the freight wagon, Sunny saw the trees skimming below give way to grassy fields, a gravel shore and then clear blue water.

"Andy!" she said. "We're over a lake and we're slowing down. Time to bail."

Moss rolled on to his front, looked down and nodded. "I can do this. Let's go."

A kilometre to the west, hidden among the tops of trees, the MANDROID plane hovered.

"What's it doing?" Donna said, staring closely at the image on screen of the Mil Mi-26 chopper dropping low and slowing as it approached the centre of the lake, its huge rotors driving white-foamed ripples outwards.

"Wait! Did you see that?" Sam exclaimed.

"It looked like two bodies fell out of the train," Arun said. "MANDROID?"

Your observation is correct, Commander. Two people

jumped from the suspended carriage into the freshwater lake below.

"Is there anybody else on the train?"

Negative.

"Then they must be our agents!" Arun said. "We've found them."

"It's blimmin' freezing!" Sunny gasped, sweeping her hands and kicking her feet to tread water.

"Well, it is an Alpine lake," Moss said, swimming up to her. "We should go for shore."

"If we don't die of hypothermia first."

Ripples from the helicopter's downwash buffeted them.

"Why is it hovering here, anyway?" Sunny asked, still watching the aircraft.

Without warning, the electromagnet disengaged. Fifteen tonnes of steel railway wagon crashed down, slammed against the surface of the lake with a tremendous splash, and bobbed for a few seconds before it slowly began to sink.

"There's your answer," Moss said, unclipping his body armour as the wave of displaced water carried him along. He began to swim towards the nearest shore.

* * *

As soon as the freight wagon hit the water, the two jet skis set off towards it, bouncing over the rippled waves. Each carried two divers. With a whirr of electric outboard engines, the two motor yachts followed.

14:34

"Suddenly it's getting really busy out there," Arun said from the MANDROID cockpit.

"Yeah, I saw them drop that train carriage but now you've got a couple of boats heading towards it, even though it sank," Sam said.

"Should we even care about that?" Donna said. "I want to know how we're going to pick up those two in the water without being seen by all that lot."

Arun smiled lopsidedly. "That's the easy part. Watch and learn, young Padawan. Watch and learn."

Donna sucked her teeth at him.

A small buoy dropped from the Mil Mi-26 helicopter to mark where the freight car had gone down, before the chopper ascended again and rumbled away towards the mountains.

The jet skiers arrived at the marker, adjusted their scuba equipment and all four flopped backwards into the water, swimming down towards the sunken carriage.

Shafts of sunlight lanced through the crystal waters.

The lead diver reached the door of the carriage and pressed a small block of C-4 against the lock. He motioned for the others to seek cover before detonating the explosive. *WHUMPFF!* A flash of light was followed by a muffled crump, and the remaining air inside catapulted the door open in a burst of bubbles. With the door hanging open, the divers quickly entered the wagon and began crowbarring open the wooden crates.

"Major," a shaven-headed soldier said, lowering his field glasses. "Look over there."

Savitch, standing on the lake shore, tracked where his newly promoted second-in-command was pointing. He adjusted the focus on his binoculars and saw two heads bobbing in the water. "Well, well, Zoltan. That would be the English my mole told me about," he said.

"Should I get one of the boats to run them down?" Zoltan said.

"It's tempting, but they're not important," Savitch said. "Let's not waste the time."

"What are the signs of hypothermia? Do you know?" Moss asked Sunny. His teeth were chattering while he swam.

246

"If you can still talk, you're OK," Sunny said. "We're gonna make it. It's only another two hundred metres."

"Easy for you to say." Moss stopped to look back. "They've got boats and jet skis out there. They're up to something."

"And there's nothing we can do about it, so keep swimming."

Moss rolled back on to his front to resume his breaststroke. "Whoa!" he said. "There's something down there, something big."

Sunny submerged her face for a better view – and saw something rising up beneath her at speed, before it lifted her and Moss out of the water.

"What the—" she said, spluttering in alarm.

She struggled to comprehend what had happened before she realised she was lying on top of a sleek underwater vessel, gently bowed and shaped like a manta ray with wide, curved wings gliding through the lake. It was barely below the surface, staying out of sight, but it was moving fast and carrying its rooftop passengers quickly to the shore.

14:44

Underwater, the dive teams were working with quick, well-practised movements. Gold bars were handed off from one diver to the next where they were distributed among eight ring nets. Once each net was stacked with fifty bars a balloon was inflated, tied to the draw rope and released to dart to the surface where it bobbed on top.

On reaching the shallows, the MANDROID submarine stopped, allowing Sunny and Moss to jump off and wade the rest of the way to the gravel beach. They crawled ashore and sat back, shielding their eyes from the sunlight sparkling on the water.

"What is that thing?" Moss said.

Something surged under the water, and a blue and gold multi-wheeled vehicle, shaped like a motor home, broke the surface and drove up the lakeside to park beside the two waterlogged agents. Fresh water poured off the gleaming sides.

"You have got to be kidding me," Moss said.

Sunny laughed out loud. "No way!"

Inside the MANDROID vehicle, the kids zoomed in to get their first proper look at Quinn's agents.

"You have got to be kidding me," Donna said, half delighted and half appalled.

"No freaking way!" Sam said.

"Now I know why Mr Quinn said we'd know them when we saw them," Arun said to himself.

"He gave those halfwits a job?" Sam said. "What a waste of taxpayer money."

The two boats circled on the lake, stopped to snag the balloons with boat hooks and fed the trailing cables on to winches. Each winch whirred to life and hoisted up a 600-kilogram net filled with gold bullion. The crew on board hauled in the catch and stacked it carefully, to disperse the weight evenly. When all eight shipments were aboard, the boats powered their way back to where the lorries were parked.

Once the boats had reached the shallows, Savitch's troops waded into the lake to meet them and started transferring the gold bars into the waiting 10-tonne trucks.

Opening the side door of the cab, Arun jumped down to greet Sunny and Moss, with Donna and Sam close behind.

"What are you doing here?" he said.

"I could ask you the same question," Sunny said, rising to her feet. "Although it is nice to see a familiar face, even if it is a *cute widdle baby one*."

Arun ignored Donna's guffaw behind him. "We came to take you two home. Apparently, you were in trouble and needed rescuing. Again."

"Not by you," Moss said. "As you can see, we're absolutely fine. No trouble at all."

"We can have you home in fifteen minutes. You know, warm room, dry clothes, a nice mug of hot chocolate..."

"With marshmallows and whipped cream," Sam added. Donna shot him a warning look.

"Of course, if you'd rather stay here, freezing cold and sopping wet, that's fine by us, too," Arun said. "We'll just tell Mr Quinn you're good and happy to stay."

"Wait. Quinn sent you?" Moss brightened. "He got our distress signal?"

Arun shrugged. "Must have. All I know is that he sent us to bring you back."

"In that case, sure."

"Do you have any towels in there?" Sunny asked, nodding towards the camper van.

"No."

"First-aid kit?"

"No."

"Food?"

"No."

"We're making a list of these kinds of things so we'll know what we need next time," Sam said. "You'll have to bear with us."

"We got some winter coats you can use," Donna said. "They're warm and dry. Should stop you getting sick." She unzipped her jacket and offered it to Sunny.

"Thank you, Donna. I didn't know you cared." Sunny wrapped it around her shoulders.

"I don't, but I might need a favour in the future and now you owe me," Donna said with a wink.

"Don't I get a coat?" Moss said plaintively, eyeing the coats the boys were wearing.

Arun and Sam looked at each other. "Rock-paper-scissors?" they both said at the same time.

"Here," Arun said, handing his coat to the grateful Moss. "How did you end up in that train carriage anyway, and why did they just dump it in the lake?"

"Oh, gosh," Moss said. "I nearly forgot. The train was doing a bullion run. Those blokes hijacked it, dumped the car with all the gold in the lake and now they're offloading it."

"What blokes? The ones in the helicopter?"

"Yeah, I suppose. Can we stop them?"

"I don't know about that," Sam said. "We have some very specific orders to pick you up and not do anything else."

"Although, technically, we might have broken those orders already," Donna chipped in.

Sunny half raised her hand. "Just to be clear," she said. "Special Agent Quinn sent you kids to fetch us?"

"Right," Sam said.

"But he sent us to shadow this gold, and he sent us first."

"Yeah..." Arun agreed, waiting to see where Sunny was going with this.

"So that would mean the mission to protect the gold takes precedence since it was first, and if Andy and I can't do it, then we can deputise you, right?"

"Sunny, they're just kids," Moss said.

"Yeah, I know. Sick, isn't it?"

Sam scowled as Sunny stole his line from their previous encounter.

Arun held up his hand. "Who's Savitch?" he asked. "We were told that Savitch had stolen the train."

Sunny shot a look of concern at Moss. "Ratko Savitch? The Executioner?"

"Maybe," Moss said. "Although, this seems a bit sophisticated for a thug like him."

"But even so... I'm overruling Quinn here," Sunny said. "I'm giving you new orders to stop those scumbags stealing the gold. We cannot let them get away with this."

Donna, Sam and Arun looked at each other.

"Where are they?" Arun asked.

"Other side of the lake, by the look of it," Moss said. "Couple of trucks."

"High-speed chase? With MANDROID?" Donna said. "It'd be rude not to."

"Be careful!" Sunny warned. "These are dangerous people."

Donna smiled. "We've got this."

The kids piled back into the motor home, and it reversed into the water.

"Hey, what about us?" Moss said. "Not even that hot chocolate?"

14:54

Once the last of the gold had been transferred, the two boats sped away and Savitch's mercenaries hauled the jet skis back on to their trailers and unhooked them from the SUVs.

"All the gold has been loaded on to the trucks," Zoltan reported. "We're ready to go."

Savitch nodded. "We break for the border. Once we're in Germany, the buyer will take ownership and our work is done."

He climbed into the driver's seat of one lorry while Zoltan pulled himself up into the other.

Engines roared and the two BMW X7 SUVs led the way up the track to the adjoining road with the Mercedes trucks rumbling directly behind.

Moss squelched along the path towards the lakeside property he had seen from the beach. Sunny plodded after him, leaving wet footprints on the sand.

The front door opened as they approached and an

elderly gentleman said, "*Kann ich Ihnen helfen?*"

"Police emergency," Moss said. "I need to use your telephone. Um, *polizei. Telefon, bitte.*"

The homeowner hesitated, before deciding that a burglar was unlikely to be soaking wet, speaking English and asking to call the police. He ushered in the two sopping visitors.

The mini convoy of a black SUV, two 10-tonne Mercedes Atego lorries and a second SUV barrelled north along the B311 highway, heading towards the mountains.

Five hundred metres behind, cruising at a safe distance, was a blue and gold camper van.

"You know, we could just follow them," Sam was saying, "and report back when they stop to deliver the gold."

"Yeah, but there are two lorries," Donna said. "What if they split up?"

"Donna's right," Arun said. "We need to stop those trucks before they leave Austria or try to unload the gold bullion."

"Four vehicles on a busy road doing fifty miles per hour," Sam said. "What could go wrong?"

"Plenty, which is why we'll have to be careful," Arun said.

"Fortunately, 'Careful' is my middle name," Donna said.

"Is it?" Sam said.

"No! Who'd call their kid that?" Donna laughed. "Man, you are so gullible!"

In London, Quinn's mobile rang.

He reached for it, praying it wouldn't be C asking for a debrief. It wasn't. Instead, it was an unknown number with a +43 dialling-code prefix.

"Hello?" he answered.

"Quinn? Is that you?"

Recognising the voice on the line, Quinn lowered his voice. "Moss? What are you—"

"It's complicated, sir."

"Tell me about it."

"I will, but first I need you to do something for me."

"I'm all ears."

The MANDROID motor home maintained its course, keeping up with Savitch's convoy.

Inside, Donna was studying maps on her screens. "Yo, MANDROID. What's this greyed-out line up ahead?"

That is the Schmitten Tunnel, a five-kilometre road tunnel bypassing the lake.

"Crud. That'll mean no overtaking. We gotta make our

move now."

This is a no-overtaking section of road. To cross the double white lines would be an offence and could attract police attention.

"Good! We could use some police backup right now."

I cannot condone—

"MANDROID, manual override," Arun commanded. "Donna, you drive."

"Yesssss!" Donna screamed, cracking her knuckles as a steering wheel assembled in front of her and two pedals extended from the base of her chair.

"Remember, you've got no mirrors, so use the side cameras and radar display," Sam said, shrinking down into his seat.

Donna tapped the screens in front of her to change the views to front and sides of the vehicle. "Hang on to your pants," she said. "Here we go."

14:58

Savitch kept a safe braking distance from the X7 in front and eased off the accelerator to stay within the speed limit. He was doing nothing that would attract the attention of the Federal Police. Everything had gone to plan. Everything except for the emergency services clearing the train tunnel faster than expected. That had meant triggering the avalanche as a contingency, something he would rather have avoided, not because of the loss of life but simply for the attention it drew. Still, it had done its job of distracting the authorities and he was almost done. His final stop was the tiny Bavarian town of Schneizlreuth, across the border in Germany, where the mastermind behind the operation was waiting with a truckload of cash as his payment for delivering the gold.

Two vehicles further back, Marko, the driver of the rear SUV, was getting irritated.

"There's a stupid caravan tailgating me," he muttered, glancing again at his rear-view mirror to see the blue and gold motor home filling the frame. "I'm surprised it can move that fast."

The camper van abruptly swung left, crossing the double white lines, flashed past the SUV and cut in to the gap behind the Mercedes lorry in front.

"What the—" Marko beeped his horn in annoyance. "Now I can't see past that thing."

Zoltan, driving the second lorry, checked his wing mirrors and curled his lip.

"I can't see Marko's SUV," he said to his co-driver. "Some idiot's cut him up."

"The Major won't like that. He'd better get back in formation."

"He can't. It's no overtaking and we're about to hit the tunnel."

As if on cue, the curved roof of the tunnel entrance closed in and the lorry was swallowed up in darkness.

Donna held her eyes on the Mercedes truck in front but kept glancing at the radar display to check for oncoming traffic in the opposite lane.

"There," she said, spotting a wide gap with no vehicles.

The driver of the SUV she'd overtaken, seeing the same

gap, dropped a gear and sped up, ready to overtake the annoying camper van in front.

"Gotcha," Donna said, and slammed on the brakes as hard as she could.

Unable to slow down in time, the X7 smashed into the back of MANDROID. The bonnet of the SUV crumpled like tissue paper and it bounced off, swerving to a stop.

Sam, Donna and Arun were flung forward in their seats, but held by the safety harnesses.

"What did you do that for?" Sam yelled.

"Yeah, next time, warn us," Arun said. "You could've damaged MANDROID, you know."

"Are you kidding?" Donna said. "What part of 'Mobile Armour' did you not get? It's right there in the name." She stomped on the accelerator again. "One down, three to go."

Marko screamed into the airbag, punching it to deflate it.

"Did you see that?" he shrieked. "Get the RPG out of the back, fast!"

His co-driver spilled out of the door, reached in and seized the metre-long rocket-propelled grenade launcher from the back seat. Immediately, he shouldered it, flipped up the iron sights and thumbed down the hammer.

Zoltan, in the second lorry, grabbed his radio and called Stefan, who was driving the other SUV. "Marko's down. Some stupid caravan hit him and now it's closing on me! Stefan, I need you back here now as a shield."

"On my way," Stefan responded.

The lead SUV drifted to the left, crossed over the centre lines and braked. The two lorries zipped past on the right and Stefan brought the X7 back into its lane to follow them, positioning himself in front of MANDROID, which was still gathering speed after Donna's emergency stop.

"Time to catch up," Donna said, pressing down on the accelerator.

"Uh-oh," Sam said, watching the rear-view screen and zooming in with low-light enhancement. "It looks like those guys who crashed have got a—"

FWOOOOSSHHH!!!

The RPG-7 launched its grenade; the second-stage rocket ignited, blasting it forwards at 600 miles an hour, targeting MANDROID directly in front.

15:01

Donna was about to break left but the radar showed an oncoming juggernaut in the opposite lane.

"MANDROID, duck!" she screamed.

A ripple pulsed across the caravan, from back to front. The seats, floor and chassis all dropped flat, as the body of the vehicle surged to the sides. In the blink of an eye, a U-shaped channel had formed down the centre of the motor home.

The blazing grenade whooshed down the tunnel, skimmed through the rounded groove of the MANDROID configuration and continued blazing forward until it connected with the back of Stefan's SUV.

K-CHOOM!

The ensuing fireball lit up the tunnel, scattering debris across both lanes.

The camper van resumed its original shape and crashed through the burning hulk of the X7.

Zoltan goggled at the flaming wreckage in his wing mirror.

"I don't believe it," he said. "We've lost both escorts."

"And that caravan is closing in," the co-driver said.

"We're coming to the end of the tunnel," Zoltan said. "That'll give us more space. Use the Ingram and take out the driver."

"Got it." Reaching under his seat, the co-driver brandished a stubby machine pistol.

Arun spun round in his seat and gaped at Donna. "I didn't know we could do that. Did you know we could do that?"

"No," Donna said, "I didn't know we could do that."

"I did," Sam said. "At least theoretically. I didn't have a chance to prove it, though."

"Consider it proved," Arun said. "MANDROID, you're just full of surprises."

"That leaves the two lorries," Donna said. "And they're picking up speed. How are we gonna stop them?"

"We're coming out of the tunnel," Arun said, seeing the glowing square of daylight rushing towards them.

MANDROID charged under the arched exit and on to the open road, which promptly widened into a dual carriageway.

The nearest Mercedes truck was about 500 metres in front and growing closer all the time.

Donna kept her foot firmly on the accelerator, reducing the distance. The road climbed steadily and a long curving stretch arced to the right. This meant the passenger side of the lorry in front was clearly in view and that's when the squat barrel of a suppressor fixed to an Ingram MAC-10 machine pistol appeared in the window and opened fire, emptying the 32-round magazine in less than two seconds.

Bullets sprayed across the MANDROID windscreen, bouncing and ricocheting like a swarm of angry bees.

"Yeah, I know, it's mobile armour," Arun said, before Donna could start.

"They're shooting at us!" Sam wailed.

"Then it's time to shoot back," Donna said. "MANDROID, can you take out the back tyres?"

Affirmative, Admiral.

"I don't think that's such a good idea," Sam said.

Donna sucked her teeth. "They started this."

"You missed," Zoltan said to his passenger. "I said take out the driver."

"I didn't miss," the co-driver insisted.

Zoltan handed him a fresh ammunition clip. "Hit it again."

The co-driver slammed home the clip and leaned out of the cab window once more, taking aim at the camper van behind.

A panel slid open on the roof of the blue and gold motor home, allowing an automatic cannon to emerge and lock in position. *BRAAP!* It fired a single, short burst.

The rear tyre of the laden Mercedes truck exploded and the wheel hub crashed to the asphalt, slicing through the rubber and spitting a shower of sparks.

Zoltan spun the steering wheel in a desperate attempt to control the skid but he overcompensated, making the truck slew side on. Forward momentum, plus nearly two and a half thousand kilograms of cargo, did the rest, tipping the lorry on to its side where it rolled, over and over.

"We can't stop!" Donna screamed, slamming on the brakes as the MANDROID camper van sped towards the bouncing wreck. "We're gonna hit!"

15:04

The Mercedes truck loomed large in the windscreen, darkening the cab and bearing down on them relentlessly.

WHAMM! A huge robotic arm emerged from the side of the motor home and slammed down on the road, pushing hard. At the same time, the front wheels locked, the back of the vehicle flipped and its speed carried it upwards so the cab was facing the road and the rear soared through the sky, tracing an arc neatly over the tumbling truck. MANDROID continued to pivot through 360 degrees, sailing upside down, before spinning back to upright in time for the tyres to slam back down on to the road.

"Wha-hooo!" Donna whooped in delight at the vehicular somersault.

Both Sam and Arun fought the urge to throw up, while the camper van bounced to a stop.

Following the action in his wing mirror, Savitch stared in disbelief. Not only had Zoltan's truck overturned, scattering gold bars across the highway, but a motorised caravan had somehow vaulted the wreck, revolving end over end, and landed on its wheels. For a split second, the thought of going back for the gold flashed through his mind but he pushed it away. His priority now was to deliver what he had. He pressed the accelerator down all the way and left the destruction far behind.

Sam called up several camera feeds and flashed pictures on to the front window. "Ooh, that looks bad," he said. "Should we check on the driver?"

Donna zoomed her own screen on a pile of gold bars, glittering at the side of the road. "Or at least put that gold where someone won't be tempted to nick it."

The distant wail of emergency sirens filtered into the cabin.

"MANDROID?" Arun said, "Are those...?"

Two police patrol vehicles are approaching from the south. The two wrecks in the tunnel are hampering other vehicles.

"Time to go, then. The police can deal with the gold and the casualties. We have one more truck to stop."

"Isn't it long gone by now?" Sam said hopefully.

"They have no idea what they are dealing with," Donna

said. "MANDROID, can you fire rocket engines at ground level?"

"No!" Sam cried.

Yes, I can but—

"No!" Sam insisted. "We don't have enough fuel to—"

"Do it!" Donna said. "Your Admiral commands it!"

Outside, the back of the camper rippled and pulsed, de-forming and re-forming. Two cavities opened in the bumper and a pair of silver exhaust nozzles extended – and fired.

Donna, Arun and Sam were thrown back in their seats and MANDROID accelerated away.

Arun gaped in horror as the road started to fall away and the nose began to lift off the ground.

"We need a spoiler!" Arun shouted.

A flat blade-like panel slid out on the back of the motor home, mounted at an angle to change the airflow passing over it and generate downforce. The front wheels thumped down on to the road surface again and the camper van shot up the mountain road.

Savitch continued speeding along the narrow highway as fast as he dared. The chunky lorry did not handle well and the rear wheels tended to slide as he took the tighter bends. A blue traffic sign warned of hairpin bends ahead, where the road hugged the mountainside.

Meanwhile, the MANDROID motor home streaked like a missile, weaving in and out of traffic, gaining all the while. Donna's hands and feet were busy, cranking the steering wheel and constantly adjusting the speed. Both boys gripped the webbing of their seat belts.

"We should try and get in front of the lorry and then slow down to make it stop," Sam said. "Like the police do."

"Can't we just shoot it?" Donna said, her eyes fixed on the road.

"And have it go over the edge with all that gold?" Sam said. "They'd spend years trying to find it all."

A sparkle in his wing mirror alerted Savitch to the blue and gold camper van closing in from behind.

"Again?" he muttered. "How? Who are these clowns?"

He twisted the wheel, changing lanes and swerved back again.

"Donna, you've got to cut the speed," Arun said. "He's seen us and he isn't going to let us pass."

"And we're burning too much fuel," Sam said, nervously

watching an amber display flashing. "We still have to get home."

"I can do this," Donna said, narrowing her eyes and judging speed, distance and road width.

"Can doesn't mean should," Sam said, shrinking into his seat.

Savitch continued to zigzag across the road, keeping one eye on the winding route ahead and one on the wing mirror to keep the camper van at bay. Directly in front, a flatbed truck, hauling a load of steel beer barrels, chugged uphill, blocking his way.

Seeing the opposite lane was clear, Savitch swung across the double white lines to overtake. His Mercedes lorry roared past the truck and, as it passed, Savitch drew his pistol and pumped two bullets into the driver's cab before completing the manoeuvre.

"Oh, no," Sam squeaked, watching the flatbed truck begin to drift across the road in front. It jackknifed, lurched, and the steel kegs broke loose, bouncing and trundling over the tarmac.

"We're going to hit it!" Arun screamed, shielding his face.
Donna fixed her gaze on a rolling barrel in front and

lined up the front tyres to crash into it.

KRUNNGG!

The camper van's wheels connected with the pressurised steel drum and bounced up while the barrel spun away, spraying lager over the road. With the motor home almost tipping on to its side, Donna tuned the speed and steering to execute a perfect side wheelie.

Skirting the mountain edge, the caravan stayed balanced on its nearside wheels at a 45-degree angle, allowing the steel drums to rumble beneath, before it passed the stalled truck and dropped back again on to all its tyres.

Savitch's look of triumph had turned into one of shock as he watched in his side mirror. With his attention split, he failed to notice the 18-wheeled juggernaut ahead, crossing into his lane to overtake a tractor.

"What's that up front?" Arun said, his voice rising in alarm. He stabbed a finger at the radar display showing a large blob bearing down from around the next bend.

The juggernaut driver looked up to see a 10-tonne truck appear from behind the mountain spur and come hurtling towards him, with a speeding motor home right behind.

Unable to get back in lane, he sounded the horn and braced for impact. *BEEEEEEEEEEEEEE!*

Savitch froze, caught between the HGV in front and the camper van behind.

Instinctively, he braked and yanked the steering wheel away from the oncoming 70-tonne lorry. The weight in the back shifted and the wheels spun, losing their grip. Skidding forwards, Savitch ran out of road. The truck ploughed through the crash barrier and soared over the edge and into space.

Donna, her face a mask of concentration, didn't waver for a second. She hit the accelerator and drove the motor home through the barrier, straight after it.

15:08

Arun felt his stomach lurch into his chest while Sam let out a long scream. Snowy mountain peaks scrolled up in the windscreen, followed by views of tree-covered hills undulating into the distance. It would have been a fine landscape scene except for the part where they were about to crash into it.

"MANDROID, can you catch that truck?" Donna said.

Negative for powered flight. Total weight is in excess of twelve point five tonnes, which is—

"Forget it! Switch to submarine mode. Now!"

"We're all gonna die!" Sam wailed.

"Donna! Are you out of your mind?" Arun said, making the sign of the cross.

Affirmative, Admiral, MANDROID said.

Instantly, the cabin ceiling dropped low and the consoles slid aside. MANDROID flattened itself out, manta wings extending to the sides.

"Ohh, wait. I get it! Donna, you're a genius!" Arun said, a wide grin starting to form. "Sam, stop sobbing and look!"

The long, curving wings sliced through the air, adjusted trim and, slowly but surely, started to lift the vehicle and level off its descent.

Donna remained focused. "MANDROID, can you shift to come under the truck?"

Calculating intercept course now. Shall I execute?

"Yes!"

The trailing edges of the wings lowered, sending MANDROID into a dive once more. Beneath it was the Mercedes lorry, plummeting nose first towards the ground, far below.

Twin engine bursts increased the sub's air speed and it caught up to dive in parallel with the truck. Another wing adjustment and it closed the gap in between, bumping its roof against the tyres of the lorry. As soon as contact was made, clamps slid out to secure the truck's wheels.

Savitch, pressed back into his seat and watching the approaching terrain in wide-eyed terror, felt the jolt and heard the clunk of the couplers.

MANDROID modified its configuration again, lengthening its wings to accommodate the additional weight and extending its twin tail fins. The bizarre-looking glider aircraft pulled out of the dive and changed direction to drift south.

15:23

Sunny and Moss stood in the middle of the lush meadow, close to the edge of Lake Zell. A chill breeze skated over the water.

"I'm freezing," Moss complained.

Sunny closed in and wrapped her arms around him, snuggling closer. "This should help warm both of us up," she said. "It's so romantic out here."

"I thought you were going to kill me if we got out alive."

"Only if you reminded me."

"Oops." Moss tilted his head in the direction of a familiar clattering sound. "There goes the moment," he said.

"Technically, we are still at work." Sunny let go and shielded her eyes while she watched the Austrian Air Force Black Hawk helicopter touch down in the field, its downwash flattening the grass.

A side door opened and Corporal Friedrich jumped out, followed by a dozen Jagdkommando.

"Mr Moss and Ms Patel," she said. "Fancy meeting you here, of all places."

"Yeah, not exactly how I thought my day was going to end," Moss said.

"The freight wagon is in the lake, you said?"

Sunny nodded. "Along with your colleague Mertens, I'm afraid."

"As I suspected. He set us up. And where is Savitch and the stolen goods?"

"He'll be here soon. Just give it a few minutes, fingers crossed."

Friedrich looked at her quizzically. These two English agents were odd, even by the usual British standards.

"Giselle! Over here!"

"Bianca?" Dallmann tossed her microphone to the camera operator and half ran, half slipped towards her sister, also hurrying towards her across the devastated slopes of the ski resort.

"What the heck happened out here?" Giselle said, grabbing Bianca in a fierce hug. "I thought ... the worst. And the kids?"

All around them, rescue teams and survivors milled about, giving details and receiving medical help.

"You probably heard," Bianca said. "The avalanche hit and most of us were buried in it."

"But no one died, or was seriously hurt? That's impossible."

Bianca looked away for a moment. "As everyone has said, we dug ourselves out. And we helped dig each other out."

"Giselle!" Fire Chief Janssen called over to her. "I've got someone here who wants to say something to you." He walked over, accompanied by a teenage boy.

"Go ahead," Bianca said. "We'll catch up later."

"Yes, young man," Giselle said to Toni.

"I know you have a job to do, reporting the news and telling people what happened here today," Toni said to her. "I just want you to know that there are some real heroes who stepped up today. Not just everyone you see here, who helped each other, but others, too, who helped because it was the right thing to do. Make sure you tell that to the world, OK?"

Giselle looked at Janssen with a raised eyebrow.

"What he said." Janssen chuckled. "Exactly what he said."

Friedrich leaned against a fence post while her Jagdkommando team sat themselves down on the grass.

"Are you sure those brats are going to deliver?" Moss

muttered to Sunny. "What if they screw up, or don't show to make us look bad?"

Sunny glared at him. "You don't know them like I do. If you did, you wouldn't be saying that."

One of the soldiers sprang to his feet and pointed skywards. "*Was ist das?*" he said.

The troops gathered and stared open-mouthed at the sight of an unusual aircraft approaching silently from the far side of the lake. It looked a bit like the Space Shuttle gliding down with a goods lorry on its back.

"Now, there's something you don't see every day," Moss said, manoeuvring for a better look.

"Looks like we have a welcome party," Donna said from her seat in the centre of MANDROID. "Let's come in for a water landing and dump this butthead."

Affirmative.

While the gathered personnel watched from the field, the blue and gold glider dropped lower and lower towards the lake's surface until it submerged completely, pushing up a bow wave. The Mercedes truck, anchored to the roof, looked like it was driving upon the water, carried aloft by the submarine craft below.

On approaching the shallows, the clamps disengaged

and the lorry rolled forwards up the beach to stop where a dozen sub-machine guns waited, all taking aim at it.

Savitch raised his hands as Friedrich marched up, her Glock automatic trained on him. "Finally," she said. "After twelve years on the run, you're under arrest."

Sunny pulled Moss aside and led him around the truck to where a sparkling camper van waited on the lakeshore, water running off in rivulets.

The door opened and Sam's face popped out. "Did someone order a taxi to London?" he said with a cheeky grin.

17:41

At Secret Intelligence headquarters on the South Bank of the Thames, Quinn was wrapping up his debrief to C, the head of the Secret Service.

"So if I were to summarise," C said, "your *S.T.E.A.L.T.H.* team not only completed the extraction, but also apprehended one of Europe's most wanted war criminals, recovered quarter of a billion pounds of stolen gold bullion, and rescued over a hundred civilians from near-certain death?"

"Not bad for a day's work, is it, sir?" Quinn said, looking smug.

C leaned back, appraising Quinn as if seeing him properly for the first time. "I'll be honest with you, Quinn," he said. "When you first ran this idea past me, I had my doubts – I still do – but this, this has surpassed my expectations." He gathered up the dossiers scattered on his desk. "You're free to expand your team. You'll have a budget and an office. You answer only to me. Are we clear?"

"Crystal clear, sir."

"But before you go, there's something that troubles me about all of this."

"Yes?" Quinn leaned forward.

"This man Savitch is a glorified thug. He doesn't have the brains to have conceived an operation like this, let alone execute it."

"You're thinking he had help?"

"More than that. I think there's someone behind it and Savitch is just the patsy. There's more to this than meets the eye. Mark my words."

When Quinn approached the makeshift situation room he had earlier commandeered, the babble of excited voices was unmistakeable. He glanced through the blinds and saw six empty pizza boxes stacked on a table beside drained bottles of cola.

Quinn entered with one hand behind his back and a hush fell across the room. Burgess, Sunny, Moss, Sam, Donna and Arun all looked at him expectantly.

"He said yes," Quinn said to a chorus of cheers. He brought his hidden hand round to show the bottle of champagne he had been concealing.

"We're on the team?" Moss said. "We passed probation?"

"You showed enough initiative, brains and courage,"

Quinn said. "With some proper training, you'll be half-decent field agents."

"Welcome aboard," Burgess said. "Time to open that champagne."

Quinn wandered over to where the kids were assembled. "As for you lot..."

"What's the matter, big man?" Donna said, smiling up at him. "We made you look good."

"You disobeyed my direct orders."

"And saved a lot of lives by doing so," Arun said.

"And potentially exposed yourselves – and MANDROID – in the process. There's a bigger picture here that you don't see, and it's my job to make sure we are all protected. That's why it is so important you listen to me."

"But the thing is," Sam said, "we didn't get seen, and those who did see anything are keeping quiet because they're grateful we helped them, and no one's going to believe a giant robot came to the rescue. So we can do the right thing without messing up."

"Look, Mr Quinn," Arun said, "we know where you're coming from but MANDROID wasn't made just to help rescue your agents. It's meant to help everyone and if it can't do that, then there's no point in having us around."

Donna rolled her eyes. "Why are we talking about this?

You didn't tell us who we were supposed to be helping or why. That's some crucial information you kept from us and if we had only done what you told us to do, then that gold would be long gone and a lot of people would be dead. Admit it, we did good."

Quinn sighed. "You got lucky this time, but you won't always be. Didn't you use Arun's real name, in front of strangers?"

"Don't give me that. If you'd have given us proper code names instead of stupid Spice Girls ones, maybe we'd use them."

"I've been thinking about that," Sam said. "You said before if we didn't like them, we could change them."

"Yeah," Quinn said, grateful for the change of subject.

"Let's change them, then. I think Donna should be something like Speed Racer."

Donna looked at Sam as if he were something smelly she had stepped in. "No way. I'd rather be GTA."

"Guaranteed Traffic Accident?" Quinn said.

"Grand Theft Auto, actually. Fine, how about … Overdrive?"

"Too much like overdose."

"What about Turbo?"

Arun and Sam exchanged looks of approval.

"I'll go with that," Quinn said. "Turbo it is."

"Sam, what about you?" Arun prompted. "You said you'd been thinking about this."

"Glutton!" Donna said.

"No! We can't call him that," Arun said.

"Gadget Man?" Donna tried again. "I know: Tool."

"What about Gizmo?" Quinn said.

"You're not naming me after a gremlin," Sam said. "How about Sparky, as in bright spark, spark of inspiration and it's what builders call an electrician?"

"That's good," Quinn said. "Arun?"

"I'll go with Rama. It's short for Ramanujan. He was an Indian mathematical genius. He had no training but came up with answers for problems that were thought unsolvable."

"Never heard of him," Quinn said.

"Exactly. You have now. Look him up."

"While we're here, what does *S.T.E.A.L.T.H.* stand for?" Sam asked.

Quinn smiled to himself. "I'll let you work it out. I'll tell you if you get it right."

"That isn't fair."

"Course it is," Quinn said. "I'll chuck in a tenner if you guess it."

"How about Secret Team Enabled Against Lethal THreats?" Donna said.

"Nope."

"All right," Arun said, "what about Strategic Threat Elimination And Leading-edge Technology Handlers?"

"Not even close," Quinn smirked.

"I know," Sam said. "It's Secret Team of Elite Academic Teen Heroes."

"You missed the L."

"Ohh. What is it, then?"

"How do you keep an idiot in suspense?" Quinn said.

"I dunno."

"I'll tell you later."

Donna laughed out loud at the confused look on Sam's face.

18:15

Quinn drained the last drops of champagne from his chipped mug, belched and raised his hand for quiet.

"Right, phone calls are all made, certificates printed, medals stamped and cover stories in place. Time for you kids to go home," he said.

"And what about us?" Donna said.

"Very funny. Sunny will walk you down and Moss will drive you home. Remember, you were at a sports meet all day."

"You said medals and certificates," Sam said, brightening. "I've never got one before for sport. My dad will be well impressed."

"You didn't really win it, you doughnut," Donna hissed.

"So? It's still real."

"Sam Evans," Quinn read out from the freshly printed document. "Bronze medal in table tennis."

"Cool!" Sam said.

"Donna Critchlow. Silver medal for the hundred metres sprint."

"Silver?" Donna was outraged. "What kind of cover story is that? No one's gonna believe that!"

"And Arun Lal. Gold medal for climbing."

"No way!" Donna raged. "That is a fix! A con!" She rounded on Arun. "You cheated!"

Quinn put his hand over his eyes and shook his head. Burgess came up to him. "You see, sir? Kids aren't so bad. They grow on you."

"So do verrucas," Quinn said, "and I don't like them, either."

Donna shrugged. "I am right. It's your house. How do we get in?"

"What, besides ringing the doorbell and saying 'Hello, Mum, I bunked off school' in front of two police officers?"

He paused, thought for a moment, then added, "The back door's usually unlocked when Mum's at home."

"Let's roll then. After you."

Still crouched down, Arun led the way on to the drive, through the side gate and round to the rear of the house. They huddled in the shadows, with the back garden stretched out before them. A bench outside the kitchen extension was shaded by the overhang. The door to the utility room was slightly ajar.

"Now what?" Sam whispered.

Arun was incredulous. "You carry that stuff around? Why?"

Donna shrugged. "Never know when you'll need it."

"That was awesome!" Sam said.

Donna ignored him. "What was that geezer up to anyway?" she said to Arun. "Was he trying to … kidnap you?"

Arun snorted. "No! He must've been from the school or something."

Donna cuffed him round the head. "Hello? Duh! He had a gun, you doughnut. If he's a copper, then I'm Beyoncé. Man, I can't believe you're supposed to be clever." She rose to her feet. "Come on, let's go see what the real Five-O are doing at your place."

As they approached Arun's house at 23 Mitchell Drive, Donna ducked down and indicated a silver Audi Q5, parked outside.

"See? Told you," she said. "Unmarked police car."

"How can you tell?" Sam asked.

"Because I can," Donna said. "Alloy wheels, extra mirrors, plain plates – it's all there."

"Hmm … assuming you're right," Arun said, sounding unconvinced, "what now?"

09:16

Donna, Arun and Sam raced round another corner and ducked into a front garden bordered by a tall hedge. Sam sank down, clutching the stitch in his side and heaving in great lungfuls of air.

Arun finally looked at the phone in his hand. "No way."

Smiling up at him was his own face, only a few years younger and holding an enormous ice cream.

"What's that about?" Sam asked, peering over his shoulder. "Why's that bloke got your picture on his phone?"

Donna ducked her head round the hedge and kneeled on the grass. "No sign of him," she panted. "Reckon we ditched him."

"Who was that?" Arun said, putting the phone away. "And what did you do to him?"

Donna pulled a scuffed hair conditioner bottle from her blazer pocket. "Home-made pepper spray," she said. "My own recipe. Mash up some Trini Scorpion peppers, mix 'em with my grandma's pickle, strain off the juice, and – major licks. It's good on burgers too."

hand pressed firmly in her blazer pocket.

"Police. This boy's under arrest."

Donna tilted her head. "On what charge?"

"Littering. Trespass. Who cares? I don't answer to you."

"My mum's a lawyer," Donna said. "I know my rights."

"Yeah? Well, why don't you just wind your neck in, or I'll arrest you too?"

Donna's eyes narrowed. "I want to see your warrant card."

The man glanced around to check the street was clear, before unbuttoning his jacket.

"Right here," he said, drawing it back to reveal an automatic pistol in a shoulder holster. "Now, bog off before things really get nast— *AaAAGH!*"

It was only from the corner of his eye, but Arun saw Donna's hand whip up from her pocket, heard the *pfft-pfft* of a spray bottle, and the next thing he knew the big man was doubled over with his hands covering his face, shrieking, "My eyes! My eyes!" His phone lay on the pavement at Arun's feet.

"Don't just stand there, you idiots!" Donna yelled. "Run!"

Arun snatched up the phone and tore down the road after her.

You'd be the same."

"Yeah, I suppose."

The two boys ran after the departing girl. They had almost caught her up, when a man's voice from behind bellowed, "You kids, stay where you are!"

Arun and Sam looked back to see a slab of muscle marching towards them from the direction of the school. "I've found the brat," the lump said into his phone. "I'll bring him in."

"Who's that?" Sam asked.

"I don't know," Arun replied with a shrug. "Doesn't look like a teacher."

The brute reached them, checked the phone in his hand and said to Arun, "You're Arun Lal, right?"

"Maybe," Arun said, unsure if it was meant as a question or a statement.

"You need to come with me. Just you."

"I've only just left the school grounds," Arun protested. "It's hardly truanting."

"I don't care about truanting. This is for your own safety. Now I won't tell you again," the bruiser said. "Come with me – or else."

"Who are you?" Donna asked. She came closer, pushing a frizzy lock of hair behind her ear while keeping her other a bank or something."

"Ha!" Sam scoffed. "More like *your* da— *Oof!*"

Donna's fist disappeared into his middle before he could finish. Sam doubled over and sagged to his knees, holding his wounded belly.

"You take that back! You take that back right now!" Donna shouted, standing over him.

"Can you two keep it down?" Arun said, helping Sam to straighten up. "We're in enough trouble already, skipping class, without telling the whole street we're here."

"She punched me!" Sam wailed.

"And you deserved it," Arun said, ignoring the scandalised look on Sam's face. "Now say sorry and let's go."

Donna stood with her arms folded, jaw thrust out, and glared at Sam. He looked to Arun for help but his friend's mind was elsewhere.

"All right. I'm sorry," Sam mumbled.

Donna sucked her teeth and said, "Man, why am I even bothering to help a couple of losers like you?" She marched towards the main road.

Arun hesitated, waiting for Sam to move.

"I thought we were friends," Sam said.

"We are," Arun said. "It's just – if she's right, I have to know what's going on. I can't wait until school's finished.

going on. They were plain-clothes cops, you know."

"How would *you* know that?" Sam said.

"Because I know," Donna said. She stormed off towards the stairs to the playground. "You coming?"

The two boys looked at each other for a moment, before Arun shrugged and trotted after her.

Sam stared, watching his friend disappear down the stairs. He could hardly believe it: Arun had ditched him – for a girl too. Then again, what if Donna was right and the police really were at Arun's house?

"Hey, wait for me!" he said, and hurried to catch up.

"Follow me," Donna said. "Do what I do, walk where I walk. Just don't run – that's a dead giveaway."

Donna led the way out of the Most Sacred Heart High School with practised ease, guiding the boys past the bicycle racks, round the sports hall and across the grass to the main gates, making sure to keep the hedges between them and the school building, before slipping out into the street.

Arun said nothing. Everyone knew Donna skipped classes; he just never expected to be joining her.

"Why would the police be at my house?" Arun said, giving in to curiosity.

"Beats me." Donna shrugged. "Maybe your dad's jacked

08:52

"Why are there police at your house?"

Arun blinked in response, unable to decide which was more weird: what Donna had said, or that she had spoken to him at all.

"Wuh?" was the best he could manage.

Donna gripped the lapel of his school blazer and hauled him aside. Other Year Sevens surged past in the corridor, hurrying to their classrooms for registration.

"I said, why are the feds at your house, dummy? I saw them show up just after you left."

Arun shook his head, dumbfounded. "I don't know what you're talking about."

"That's right, Donna," Sam said, sticking up for his best friend.

"How would you know?" Donna sneered.

"Let me go," Arun said, trying to pull away. "We'll be late for registration." The corridor was almost clear.

"Listen," Donna said, "you can go to class and be teacher's pet, or you can come with me and suss what's

IT'S JUST ANOTHER ORDINARY DAY.

UNTIL IT ISN'T.

S.T.E.A.L.T.H.
ACCESS DENIED

Read on for an extract of the explosive first book.